THE ROOFTOP GARDEN

THE
ROOFTOP
GARDEN

MENAKA RAMAN-WILMS

NIGHTWOOD EDITIONS

Nightwood Editions
P.O. Box 1779
Gibsons, BC VON 1V0
Canada
www.nightwoodeditions.com

COVER DESIGN: Angela Yen
TYPOGRAPHY: Carleton Wilson

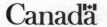

Nightwood Editions acknowledges the support of the Canada Council for the Arts,
the Government of Canada, and the Province of British Columbia through
the BC Arts Council.

This book has been produced on paper certified by the FSC.

Printed and bound in Canada.

LIBRARY AND ARCHIVES CANADA CATALOGUING IN PUBLICATION

Title: The rooftop garden / Menaka Raman-Wilms.
Names: Raman-Wilms, Menaka, author.
Identifiers: Canadiana (print) 20220261776 | Canadiana (ebook) 20220261784 |
    ISBN 9780889714380 (softcover) | ISBN 9780889714397 (EPUB)
Classification: LCC PS8635.A4614 R66 2022 | DDC C813/.6—dc23

They play the game where they are the last people on earth. They are in a forest, and it is almost dark, and they have to find shelter and make dinner. Nabila crushes flower petals with a stick. The smell is warm and sick-sweet and makes her sneeze.

Matthew is in charge of shelter, but he just squats behind the rose bush and pushes dirt around with his finger.

Nabila is still trying to figure out what has happened. Either there was an earthquake and entire cities have fallen into the cracks, or the North Pole melted and the oceans have flooded the world. They must be on one of the few islands left. Nabila adds some dried leaves to the flower petals and they crumble and almost turn into powder.

She hears a noise above them and drops her stick spoon. "Plane!" she calls over to Matthew, and he makes room for her to huddle next to him behind the rose bush. There's a bit of an overhang, and though they have to be careful not to touch the branches, the rose bush keeps them secret from the skies.

They have to hide from planes that pass above them. That's one of the rules.

When the coast is clear, Nabila goes back to making dinner. "Bring me some mud," she tells Matthew, so he spits twice into a handful of dirt and mashes it up, then places it next to her petals and leaves. When she mixes in the mud it becomes a brown paste, sticky like syrup, and it stirs like the dough of something her father would bake.

They listen to the familiar noises from the city below: groaning sea monsters, shifting earth plates, underwater dragons coming up to surface.

Dinner will be ready soon.

M atthew had disappeared. It had been three months now since she'd last seen him, the day he showed up unannounced at her lab wearing a sweater that was too small so that his wrists stuck out the ends of the sleeves. He'd sat down on a stool on the other side of the bench and stared at a jar filled with immobilized krill. "I'm supposed to leave the country," he'd said to her, and at first she couldn't quite figure out why he was telling her. It was only afterwards, after he'd stood up and walked out of the room, that she felt she maybe could have said more.

Once he'd left, she'd seen that he'd left a crumpled gum wrapper on the stool. It must have fallen out of his pocket, and she left it there, glanced at it all afternoon whenever she passed. It had been strange to see Matthew again. And she'd never expected he'd come to the university.

Nabila was measuring how kelp grew in different water temperatures. She had seven canisters of clear glass lined up, the water inside kept at steady rates by heating and cooling systems, pipes pushing tiny bubbles of air through. The water in each canister was set to a different temperature, each one getting progressively warmer than the one beside it. That afternoon she'd started as usual with the first one, documenting the length of each plant, the colour, and making her way down the line. She did this every other day, noting any changes, noting anything out of the ordinary.

That day, she remembered thinking that gum wrapper was the thing out of the ordinary. Every time she passed the stool she felt compelled to look at it, to picture Matthew sitting there, his hands in his lap, his head swivelling around at the sound of the thermometer beeping or bubbles rushing. "What should I do?" he'd said a few times, and she hadn't understood why he'd come to her with this question, why he'd insisted on sitting there in the middle of her research project. Even now, when Nabila thought back to it, she remembered how out of place Matthew had been, how strange it was to see him in her world at the university. How he'd wanted an instant answer in a room designed for things taking time.

Now she was walking along a street with foreign graffiti on the walls of foreign buildings. It was a Monday, which meant it was a day she was supposed to be measuring her kelp. She was supposed to be in her lab surrounded by tanks of water. Instead, there would be an eager undergrad stepping in, and though Nabila had shown the undergrad everything in detail, she was still worried that her absence would create inconsistency. She'd never left in the middle of an experiment before. It made her feel negligent, but she knew she didn't really have a choice. She knew she needed to be in Berlin.

It was sunny, though not that warm; a few orange leaves caught up in the wind on the sidewalk. Nabila pulled her suitcase along the cobblestones and the wheels kept getting stuck on edges. It was early morning and the streets were quiet, some takeout containers and a vomit stain the only evidence of people having passed. There was a smell of greasy food, small crabgrasses clinging to bits of dirt between the sidewalk cobblestones. She stepped around the plants and moved down the street quickly. She kept an eye on the street numbers.

Her flight from Toronto had been delayed, and while they sat on the tarmac for nearly an hour she'd stared out the window, worried about missing her connecting flight and thought about the mental state of Matthew, the malleability of him. That must have had something to do with it, she thought, must have been at least part of the reason why things had happened the way they did. He'd always been on the verge of being convinced.

Nabila passed a parkette with some graffitied benches, and then she saw it, the tree sticking out of the building. The woman she had spoken to had said the place was unique. The tree's trunk emerged from the middle of the roof, and the branches fanned outward, still filled with orange and yellow leaves. The war tree, she'd called it. Said it had survived both wars and nobody had wanted to cut it down when the street was being developed.

The front of the building had glass windows filled with books. Most were in English, and as Nabila approached she saw folk tales and gardening guides and scientific manuals. There were plants, too, in round pots suspended from the ceiling in macramé hangers, their vines and leaves interspersed with the book covers. *Café Arboretum,* read the sign above the door. Nabila went inside.

She saw bookshelves and an espresso bar, and the woman behind the counter was singing along to the radio. "Hallo," she called over in Nabila's direction.

"Oh, hi. Are you Tierney?"

"You found her."

Nabila walked over, extended her hand. Her suitcase made a loud noise on the wooden floor. "I'm Nabila. We've been emailing. About the room."

"Oh, hey." Tierney took off her apron, ran around to the other side of the bar and caught Nabila's fingers. Her handshake was light. It wasn't really a shake at all, Nabila thought, more like a touch of their palms. Tierney smiled and something on her tooth sparkled.

"You made it, girl. I was wondering."

"I've never been to the city before," Nabila said, then realized it wasn't really an explanation. She shuffled her feet.

"You find the place okay?"

"Oh yeah. Can't miss the war tree."

Tierney grinned. It was a diamond, Nabila realized. A tiny diamond glued to her front tooth. Tierney reached up and released her hair from its ponytail, shaking it out across her shoulders. Nabila caught the smell of coconut.

"Come on. The tree's in the backroom. I'll show you the whole place."

Nabila grabbed the handle of her suitcase and followed Tierney across the floor. Besides the espresso bar along one wall, the rest of the room was covered in shelves. There were books and succulents, a long vine with thick leaves that snaked along the ceiling. In the corner were a few chairs and a couple of tables, empty. Nabila saw a stain from a coffee cup on one of the wooden surfaces as she walked past.

Tierney led her through a small hallway with a single light bulb hanging from the ceiling. Then the space opened up again, into a room that was filled with sunlight. "Here we go," Tierney said, and Nabila got her first glance of the tree, standing right in the middle of the room. It was wide, a few feet across. The bark was thick and dark, with rigid grooves. There were shelves on the walls holding more books and English ivy stretching across them, a couple of chandeliers hanging from the ceiling, but the tree took over the room. There was a hole cut in the roof, and the trunk rose right through it. On the other end, its roots sprawled a foot in all directions and then disappeared into the floor.

"Not bad, right?" Tierney said.

Nabila nodded.

"Fiction's out front, and back here I've got history and science," she said, walking along the length of a shelf and running her fingers across the spines. "And travel, horticulture. Sociology. There aren't too many English bookstores around here so we kind of have to do it all."

"It's great," Nabila said.

She followed Tierney through the room, blinking against the brightness of the sunlight. The far wall had large windows and a glass door. Tierney opened it and led her into a garden walled in by a tall fence. "Careful, there's thorns. Everything else is pretty much gone now. A few months ago, this place was alive. Purple and yellow flowers, raspberries, but now it's all in retreat. And here we've got the stairs to the next floor. Need a hand?"

"No thanks," Nabila said, and then realized that the staircase wasn't anything more than a fire escape leading up from the corner of the garden, rusted to a deep shade of orange-brown.

"This is the only staircase?"

"Well, there's one from the front room too, but I try to keep that door locked, with the café right there. You know. Don't want randoms going up."

"Right."

The stairs shook as they climbed, and Nabila carefully lifted her suitcase in front of her, conscious of the shift in weight. She tried not to touch the rusted railings. Ahead of her, Tierney walked up without even looking at the steps. She took a key from her pocket, unlocked the door at the top.

"Come on in, girl," she said, holding the door open. "Your room's on the left. My room's this one on the right and then the bathroom and kitchen are down the hall. There's a cupboard with towels, and sheets are already on the bed. Wi-Fi password is on the desk. Need anything else?"

"I don't think so."

Tierney pushed ahead and unlocked Nabila's room. There was a single bed, a wardrobe, a desk and chair facing the window overlooking the street. She turned on the light and everything glowed faintly yellow. A framed picture of irises hung on one wall, a diagram of a tree's root system on another.

"This key's for the outside door, this one's for your room. I know you booked four nights, but let me know if you want to extend. Things are pretty quiet this time of year."

"Okay. Thanks."

Nabila put her suitcase down in the corner and walked over toward the window. Two teenagers were running down the sidewalk, speaking loudly in German. She heard Tierney's feet shift on the floor behind her.

"I'll let you unpack, but I'll be downstairs if you need anything. Like a coffee. You probably need a coffee soon, right?" She grinned and her tooth diamond caught the yellow light. "Just let me know. I'll make you something."

"Sure. Thanks again," Nabila said and then Tierney was gone, just like that, and she was left alone in the room. She listened to the clang of Tierney's footsteps as she walked back down the fire escape.

Nabila opened her suitcase but didn't really unpack. She took out a change of clothes and laid them on the bed, then walked down the hall to find the bathroom. It was a long narrow room, the sink, toilet and shower all lined up in a row, one after the other. She washed her face, dried herself off with her sleeve because she'd forgotten to grab a towel. Her eyeliner had smudged beneath her lids and she tried to wipe it away.

The kitchen was small, the fridge and stove surrounding a tiny table. One of the walls jutted out, and she realized it was where the war tree must be. They'd sealed it off from the second floor. She knocked on the wall and the sound came back hollow.

Berlin was a flat city. She knew it had been built on a swamp, and they had to actively pump water out of some places to keep them dry, to keep them from flooding. She imagined the ground beneath the pavement soggy. She imagined the roots of the war tree stretching down into the earth, pale and tubular, until they met water.

This was the city that Matthew was coming to. He probably didn't even know those details about its geography, and yet here they were.

Nabila walked back to her bedroom and shut the door. She took off her socks and pulled on a fresh pair, sat on the bed cross-legged. She checked her phone, saw there were no new messages, then put it away. She wanted to go somewhere, do something, but she knew that for now she had to wait. Instead she thought about her kelp in their glass canisters of the basement laboratory, swaying slightly in the water. Even in isolation, she imagined the plants moving as if pushed by currents.

M atthew hasn't heard about how cars are heating up the world, so Nabila tells him. She says it's why the ice at the North Pole is melting, and the more that everyone drives, the hotter everything gets. Soon the ocean will rise and swallow up Vancouver.

She can only tell him things like that when Tara Lynn isn't listening, because sometimes Matthew gets scared. Then Nabila gets in trouble. So she waits until Tara Lynn is reading baby books with Samir on the other side of the rooftop and then she and Matthew duck behind their hedges. It's only when they are in their secret forest hideaway that Nabila tells him things like that.

"This is why our forest really is on top of a building," Nabila says one day. "Water flooded the city and everybody had to leave and then trees just started growing over all the empty buildings. Their roots probably poked through the concrete and started breaking all the glass."

Matthew is eating his after-school snack, a chocolate chip granola bar. He stops chewing and looks at her. A piece of granola sticks to his lip.

"Where did everyone go?" he asks.

"Maybe some of them didn't make it. The rest went into the mountains."

"Why didn't we go with them?"

Nabila shrugs. "We got left behind."

Matthew's eyes get wide. "The forest is eating the city and we're stuck on a building," he says quietly, his mouth still full.

Nabila plants seeds so they can grow food. She digs six small holes in a row, drops in pretend seeds, then covers them back up with dirt. She realizes that pieces from the granola bar would make perfect seeds.

"Maybe we tried to go too," she says as she reaches over and picks up a few bits that Matthew dropped on the ground. "But we got stuck. There was too much water."

She digs new seed holes and places granola in each one. Matthew squeezes the last bit of the bar out of the wrapper and hands it to her, and she breaks it into little bits and lays them on the earth.

"Don't waste the chocolate chips."

He reaches over and picks them out and drops them on his tongue.

Tara Lynn always remembers that chocolate is Matthew's favourite. Every Friday she brings them an after-school treat, and Nabila notices that the treats always have chocolate.

Matthew has only been coming home with them for a few weeks. It started in mid-September; they were walking home one day and Tara Lynn noticed Matthew. He was walking up ahead of them, alone. Nabila wondered why he was allowed to go places on his own, and Tara Lynn said that they should invite him to join them.

So the next day, when Nabila came out of school to meet Tara Lynn and Samir at the edge of the teachers' parking lot, Matthew stood there, too. Tara Lynn handed them both Tupperwares of apple slices, and they walked home together.

Tara Lynn said she had arranged for him to stay with them after school until his sisters arrived to pick him up. Nabila wanted to say no, but her brother could barely just walk so at least she'd have somebody her own age to play with.

Matthew isn't in the regular grade three class like Nabila. He is in the two-three split, which everyone says is where they put the smart grade twos and the stupid grade threes. Nabila had never talked to him before. But she knows that some kids make fun of him because one time at recess he had picked up a frog and it had peed on his hand.

Matthew turned out to be okay. When Nabila talks, he mostly just listens. She figured out that if she plans a game, he'll play it. If she makes up rules, he'll follow them.

That's why they always play the forest game. It's Nabila's favourite. Her mother is a scientist and teaches Nabila a lot about the environment, including all the ways the world is changing because it's getting warmer. Humans cut down too many trees, and trees are the things that make the air pure. Then humans drive too many cars, and car pollution turns the air to poison. Glaciers melt and flood the ocean. Turtles swallow plastic bags because they look like jellyfish.

Matthew doesn't seem to know any of that stuff, so while they play, Nabila tries to explain things to him.

He scares easily. He listens to her with his mouth hanging open, his eyes round and too-pale blue. When she tells him there is a big hole in the sky over the South Pole, he worries everyone will die when outer space rushes in.

They always go to the rooftop after school. Tara Lynn and Samir sit in the gazebo and Nabila takes Matthew to the garden to play. There is a small row of hedges, some rose bushes and a few plants that have big leaves and don't grow very tall. There are also flowers. Then there are the two sandbar willows that tower over everything else. Nabila loves the trees: they have long, thin branches that stretch up toward the sky, and the leaves hide their forest from everyone else. That's where she and Matthew play, in the dirt between the plants where nobody else can see them.

After an hour, they all go down to the apartment lobby where Matthew's sisters wait to pick him up. The sisters both go to high school and one has blonde hair and the other has pink, and they never hug Matthew, just sometimes touch his shoulder.

Once he leaves, they go back up to their apartment and Tara Lynn finishes making dinner while Nabila does her homework. She sits on one side of the kitchen table, and Samir sits on the other in his high chair, eating peas or bits of chicken and sometimes rubbing it on his face to make Nabila laugh. Tara Lynn leaves when their parents arrive, just before dinner. Then Nabila's father pours two glasses of wine and a glass of grape juice before he changes out of his suit. He takes his wine to the bedroom, and comes out a few minutes later in jeans and a t-shirt. Nabila's mother still wears her work clothes and they all sit at the table and eat together. Nabila sits between her parents and takes little sips of her grape juice because that's how her mother drinks her wine. Samir sits opposite her in his high chair, fussing, because it is almost bedtime.

Matthew's father doesn't live at home. Nabila knows that, but she doesn't know why. It's just Matthew with his sisters and mother, and his mother works almost every evening, so Matthew says that they eat a lot of pizza. Nabila only gets to have pizza at birthday parties.

When the granola seeds are all covered in dirt, Nabila decides that they will make a bowl lined with waxy leaves to collect rainwater. Then they can water their plants, she tells Matthew, so he starts digging a hole with his fingers in the earth between them.

When the seas begin to rise, Nabila's mother tells her, freshwater will become very precious. There won't be much of it left. They have to make sure they don't waste the bowl of rain, Nabila thinks, and then notices that Matthew is watching her, waiting for what she will say needs to be done next.

Tierney smoked a cigarillo on the bridge over the railway every night. She lit it when the train to Potsdam rolled past, and she had a rule that it had to last until the next train going to the Hauptbahnhof came by. She told Nabila that one time she'd seen a man riding on top of a carriage, lying flat and holding onto the edges of the roof. Another time, kids had left something tied to the rail to see what would happen and then came back after the train had passed but couldn't find it.

Nabila had slept for most of the day. She'd woken up in the middle of the afternoon, still wearing her airplane clothes, the window casting a square of sunlight across her belly. People were out, and she could hear them on the street talking, could hear bicycle bells ringing. She'd gotten up and showered and then had gone downstairs to ask Tierney where she could get groceries. Out on the sidewalk, the noise was overwhelming. The day had warmed up enough that she didn't need her gloves. The sky was bright so she put her sunglasses on and walked straight down the road, tried not to focus on the unfamiliar sounds of the language.

She bought cheese and bread and apples, vanilla yogurt sold in a glass jar. She didn't speak to anyone, counted out the exact change when the cashier pointed to her total on the screen.

She missed her lab. There was a kind of peace in being surrounded by tanks of water, and that's what she was used to, where she'd come to be comfortable. She felt out of place in this loud city filled with graffiti and sunshine. She went back to her room and stayed there.

Tierney had found her a few hours later in the kitchen, sitting at the table in front of her empty sandwich plate.

"The café's closed," she announced as she walked in, a bottle of red wine in her hand. She sat down in the chair opposite Nabila and put the wine on the table between them.

Nabila smiled, and then thought she should maybe say something, but couldn't figure out what it would be.

"There's always a mix of interesting people, oh man," Tierney went on almost immediately. "This one guy bought a book on the Balkans because he was planning a trip there." She got up from the table and started pulling wine glasses out of a cupboard. "He wants to see this abandoned airfield there. Apparently his uncle or somebody was a pilot and he had to leave his plane and it's still just sitting there, along with other planes, in this old hangar. And he's going to travel there and take pictures of the plane for his aunt so she can see them before she dies. Isn't that crazy?"

"That is cool."

"I mean, how many people travel for reasons like that?" Tierney opened the bottle and filled two glasses almost to the brim. "The first glass should always be the biggest glass," she laughed, and Nabila laughed a bit, too. "It's really cheap stuff, so you've got to drink it without tasting much. Want some crackers with it? I think I have some cheese."

Tierney opened the fridge and took out a jar of olives and a block of white cheese and laid them in the middle of the table without a plate. "Grab us a knife, will ya?" she said while pulling over a chair to reach the cupboard above the fridge. "In the drawer beside the sink. Over there."

"Uh, okay." Nabila got up from the table and opened the drawer. She was starting to understand just how quickly things happened with Tierney. She remembered how when she'd first emailed about the room last week to see if it was available, Tierney had sent her a note back within an hour, along with a map and a list of tourist sites in Berlin.

Tierney jumped down from the chair with a box of crackers in her hand and placed them next to the knife Nabila had left on the table. Then she took a seat and pulled her legs up on the chair to sit cross-legged. "So," she said as she picked up her wine glass and took a long sip. "How was the first day?"

Nabila took a seat and had a drink, too. It was sweet as juice. "I walked around a bit and got to know the area. It's nice. And the war tree is easy to spot so I didn't get lost."

"Isn't it awesome?" Tierney took another long sip. "They built the whole place around it. I love it. Apparently its roots spread out beneath the entire building and yard, and even past that. I guess roots go pretty far."

"It's probably looking for other trees."

"What?"

"It's how they talk." Nabila tapped the stem of her glass with her nails. Tierney was watching her. "So," she said, "there's this forester who studies trees, and he believes that they use their roots to talk to each other."

"Talk to each other?"

"Well, communicate. Share information."

"Oh. Neat."

"Yeah."

There was a pause, and Nabila took another drink, and Tierney smiled. Her tooth diamond sparkled.

"I study seaweed," Nabila said, as if to explain.

"Seaweed? Oh. Cool." Tierney reached over and cut off a slice of cheese. "We only have lakes and the river around here. Unless you go up to the Baltic, or the North Sea." She pointed to the left. "Then you can see the ocean. It's cold, but you can still swim for a bit."

"Sounds nice."

Tierney kept talking, and Nabila listened. She ate some olives and cut a piece of cheese and drank the wine in gulps. On the other side of the table, Tierney ate crackers by the handful.

She'd only had the café for the last year, she told Nabila, had bought it from an Irish woman who had moved to Berlin for love, but was then getting divorced. Tierney liked making coffee and talking to people. That was her favourite part of the job.

Nabila was glad that she didn't have to say much. She started to feel better, like she was finding her footing on this side of the globe and was able to stand without teetering. It was easy to just sit and listen, and she liked the sound of Tierney's voice, the familiarity of her North American accent. Tierney was from California, but had moved to Berlin seven years ago. "Also for love," she said, left it at that.

When Tierney got up for her nightly cigarillo, she invited Nabila along. It was cooler in the early evening, and quiet, and those things, along with the wine, helped Nabila relax. They passed a park with a playground, and she noticed old logs that had been made into kid-sized benches. There was an ice cream shop, and even though it was too cold for ice cream, a few people were lined up outside.

A pedestrian bridge ran over the railway tracks, and they stood in the middle of it against the railing, Tierney dropping bits of ash on the ground far below. The sun had set, but the horizon was lit up in the distance in a pink haze. Taffeta, Tierney called the colourful clouds, but Nabila told her that it was pollution.

"So are you just sightseeing in Berlin?" Tierney asked then, and Nabila froze for a moment, trying to figure out which version of the truth would do best. Tierney offered her a drag on the cigarillo and she accepted, taking the moment to think.

"I'm meeting my boyfriend," she finally said, after what seemed to her like a long pause. "He's been travelling for a bit." She handed back the cigarillo and their hands touched briefly, and Tierney's fingers were warmer than she expected. "I really wanted to see Berlin though, so I'm here for a few days, and then we're meeting and going home."

"Nice," Tierney nodded, and before she could ask any more details, Nabila started talking about the city's museums, about which ones she wanted to see.

Tierney began telling her about the Neues Museum, about how it had been abandoned for years after the war and trees had grown up the staircase, but Nabila was focused on keeping her face calm, her breathing steady. She knew her story made sense, but it still felt strange to say it. She watched the glowing end of Tierney's cigarillo, nodded as she kept speaking.

"There it is," Tierney said suddenly, and Nabila stood up straight. "See it? Coming around the corner?"

Nabila followed her finger and could see the engine of a train in the distance, the light on its front spotlighting the track ahead. The train ran toward them and then underneath them, and the bridge shook. Nabila could feel it in her teeth.

The cigarillo was right down to Tierney's fingers, her nail resting against a lipstick stain. When all the cars had passed, she rubbed the glow out against the side of the railing. Then she stepped on the end.

"That's the best way to finish a day," she said, and looked out toward the horizon, sighing.

Nabila took a step away from the edge of the bridge, was ready to leave, but Tierney wasn't quite done. She pushed herself up so that she could sit on the railing, and then swung one leg over so she was straddling it. She looked like a teenager, Nabila thought. She was sure Tierney was older than her, but there was a carelessness in her manner, an openness to danger that made her seem as if she were just discovering her freedom in the world.

"Aren't you afraid you'll fall?"

"I'm not scared of heights," she said.

Tierney sat there for a while, swinging her legs back and forth. Nabila watched her. Another train approached, and they both looked down as it passed, saw Tierney's boot dangling in the air above it. Nabila could smell exhaust and a new crispness in the air, a hint of frost. Then Tierney hopped back down onto the bridge.

"So, what's next?" she asked. "You feel like going somewhere? There are some places down in Kreuzberg that are pretty fun. Doesn't take too long to get there on the S-Bahn."

"Well," Nabila said. The wine was starting to wear off and she remembered how she didn't have Wi-Fi out here, that if Matthew had sent her a message she wouldn't see it until she was back in her room. She was suddenly worried that she'd miss something. "Actually," she said, looking over at Tierney, "I'm still pretty tired. I think I'm kind of jet-lagged."

"Oh." Tierney's face fell a bit, but then she picked herself right back up. "Of course, girl. Let's get you home."

They walked back the way they came, but things looked different in the dark. Nabila couldn't quite tell where she was, and she didn't like that, didn't like that she wasn't sure of directions. The night smelled like smoke and gasoline and food, the last whispers of warm weather before things started to disappear beneath the cold. She felt disoriented.

It was hard to see the war tree in the dark, but she could hear it, was aware of the leaves rustling high above the building as Tierney unlocked the door. They stepped inside, and Tierney went behind the espresso bar, pushed open the door to the small kitchen in the back. "I'll just be a second," she said. "You like cake, right? I've got half of this great orange-cream vanilla one. It's too old to sell, but it's still good to eat."

Nabila stood in the middle of the quiet, dark room. She noticed the aroma of coffee, but also earth, she realized, of the dirt in the planters. She breathed it in, and felt something settle inside of her. She thought maybe she could bring one of the plants into her room.

There was a thump from somewhere inside the building, and Nabila wondered if Tierney had dropped the cake. But a moment later Tierney emerged from the door, pastry box in hand.

"Was that you? That noise?" she asked.

"I thought it was you."

They looked at each other for a second, and then they heard it again. It was a dull thud, not too loud, but clear enough in the silence of the café. It was coming from the backroom.

Tierney left the cake on the counter and stepped toward the hall-way. Nabila followed. The lights were still off. The calmness that she'd felt for a moment had faded, had been replaced with an attentiveness, a need to be alert. She stayed directly behind Tierney.

The room at the end of the hallway was dark except for a narrow beam of light that came through the window on the closed garden door. They took a few steps in and then stopped again. It was cooler in there. Nabila tried to make out shapes in the darkness, and after a moment she could see books, and then the tree in the middle.

She looked at Tierney, and Tierney shrugged. They took a few more steps; the floorboards creaked beneath their feet and suddenly there was a rustling, a scratching on the floor or the wall. A shape appeared in the beam of light and immediately disappeared. Then there was something above them, swooping over their heads.

"What the hell?" Nabila ducked.

Tierney reached for the light switch and everything became golden yellow, and Nabila couldn't see for a few seconds. She blinked and blinked. She could hear the swooping continue though, could tell that something was flying to the other end of the room and then back toward them.

"Is it a bat? It sounds like a bat."

"It's a bird," Tierney said. It flew around her, just missing her outstretched hand. "I left the garden window open this afternoon since it was so nice."

Nabila could see the wings now. It was small, pale brown with a black beak and black eyes. As she watched, it flew across the room to the garden door and right into the windowpane. It fell to the ground, but picked itself up and stumbled on the floor for a minute. Then it started flying around the room again.

"We should open the door," Nabila said, but when she began walking across the room, the bird just flew faster. Its movements were sporadic, dipping down and then up, circling the tree over and over again. It headed toward her, and Nabila ducked, felt the rush of air beneath its wings.

"Let's let it land," Tierney said.

They both stood still, but the bird didn't stop. It kept swooping around and almost hit the crystals on a chandelier.

"It's not stopping," Nabila said, and started again to make her way toward the door. It would be easy for them to help it, if it would just stay still. She moved slowly, but the bird kept its pace, circling overhead. When she reached a hand out to grab the door handle, the bird flew quickly above her and then dove straight down toward the windowpane on the top half of the door. There was a loud smack as it hit the glass and fell to the floor. This time it didn't get up.

"Is it okay?" Tierney whispered from behind her.

Nabila hovered over the bird and then bent down. She could see a smudge of blood on the floor next to its head. Its wing moved a bit, and Nabila touched it softly, stroked its feathers. She could feel its frantic heartbeat. Its entire body quivered beneath her fingers. Then it stilled.

Tierney appeared behind her, put a hand on her shoulder. "We should take him outside." She stepped past Nabila and opened the door, and Nabila could feel the coldness of the night rush in. She cupped her hands beneath its wings, and felt a hollowness grow in her belly. The bird didn't stir. There was now blood and bird poo on the floor beneath it, and she waited a second, hovered the body just off the boards, just to be sure. Then she carried him out into the garden and laid him at the base of a fencepost.

"You should wash your hands," Tierney said.

Nabila nodded.

They went back inside and wiped off the floor and then Nabila cleaned her hands in the downstairs kitchen sink. Her fingers were tingling. She thought of the smell of the garden earth, of the bird slowly becoming a part of it. She pictured his tiny hollow bones sitting in the soil after the rest of him had decomposed.

"Should we have buried him?" she asked Tierney as they were turning off the lights. She was suddenly worried that it had been indecent to just leave him there. She glanced back toward the yard.

"I wouldn't worry." Tierney shook her head. "Some animal will probably find it, might make a meal out of it," she said. "By morning, it should be long gone."

Nabila had forgotten to close her curtains. She woke up and it was still dark, the streetlights shining through, and for a moment she thought it was sunlight. There were night noises outside: a dog barking, an ambulance. She heard someone singing a song in the distance.

She was worried about the war tree. The bark had seemed healthy when she'd touched it, but she wondered if it was lonely. Trees in a forest grew close together so that they could protect each other, so that if one tree was having trouble, the others would use their roots to share sugar. They'd grow their canopies right next to one another so they could stay sturdy during windstorms. The war tree, though, didn't have any of that security. One infection or strong storm might do it in.

Nabila got up from her bed and stood by the window. She put her face close to the glass and could hear the rustling of the tree's leaves above her, knew that its roots were probably stretching and searching. She wondered if it had made contact with the trees in the parkette across the street, their roots twining together beneath the hard-packed soil under the road pavement. She wondered, when the other trees all around it had died, if it had understood that it was now on its own.

She sat back down on her bed, then decided against it, got up and went to the kitchen for a glass of water.

The hallway was colder than her bedroom and she wished she'd put on socks. She turned on the kitchen light and filled a glass from the tap, then sat down at the table. The building was old and it would creek when the wind blew, when a radiator in another room turned on. Out the window, the sky was clear and she could see stars.

She was supposed to meet Matthew within the next two or three days. It wasn't clear exactly when, but it should be soon, and she needed to wait for him to contact her. But she'd been waiting for a message for a few days now, and she didn't think she'd be able to focus on anything else. The idea of seeing him again was looming at the back of everything. It would be there if she went to a museum, if she sat and had a croissant and a cup of tea in a shop. Lurking.

There was a noise like a chair scraping on the floor, and Nabila realized that it was coming from the hollow wall, the tree chamber. She got up and put her ear up against the wall and listened. There was creaking, some gentle cracking.

Trees could use those sounds to communicate, she'd read. Sometimes, if a tree was too dry, the cracking would move through the bark and vibrate like vocal cords. As if the tree were screaming. Nabila took in a deep breath, put her hand against the wall, too. She wondered if the plants downstairs made things any easier for the tree. She figured probably not. But roots could lay dormant for years, she knew, so maybe somewhere in the ground there was still growth from some of the other trees, and they were just waiting, preparing for when conditions were ideal. Then they would emerge again.

Nabila stepped back to the table, finished her water, then put the glass in the sink. She returned to her room and got back into bed. The idea of the tree silently screaming had bothered her, and she thought about how oblivious everyone in the café really was, how maybe only the plants on the shelves or in the garden knew what was really going on. She lay there for a while thinking about it, closed her eyes, then opened them and stared at the ceiling. She imagined what the war tree would look like in the dark, swaying above the roof, the trunk in the empty room surrounded by books. Then she thought of the dead bird at the base of the fencepost, its eyes being eaten by ants.

Tomorrow she'd call her undergraduate, she thought. She'd get her to take a video of the canisters, and Nabila would check on the kelp herself, would make sure her seaweed was doing okay. She'd make sure that the oxygen settings were correct, that the colour of the plants seemed appropriate.

These thoughts finally let her relax.

There was that year that they'd spent in the garden together. Whenever she thought of Matthew, that's what she remembered, sitting between the rose bushes and cedar hedge, mixing pretend food with sticks. Nabila remembered the way the soil used to feel, cool, slightly moist, how it would leave imprints on her kneecaps. She remembered the expansive world around her, the trees, the tops of other buildings and then Matthew, small and pale, blinking rapidly as she explained things.

The forest game hadn't existed before him. She'd thought of it while the two of them were there together, had figured out the details and suddenly it had all made sense. He'd arrived, and trees were reclaiming the concrete. The ocean was filling the streets and they were surviving.

She'd tried to continue the game after he was gone, but things had been more tied to Matthew than she'd realized. It didn't work without him. She'd just sat there in the dirt.

After that year in the garden, they'd stayed on the fringes of each other's lives. They'd gone to the same school, but were never in the same class, never talked if they passed each other in the hallway. Nabila did choir and volleyball and the science olympics, and Matthew didn't seem to do much of anything. He never volunteered for sports day, was never picked to read poems at an assembly. She saw him walking home sometimes, his shoulders slouched, his mouth hanging slightly open as if his nose was stuffed.

In high school, she'd started to hear stories about Matthew: he'd gotten drunk at a party and someone had punched him for being an idiot, he'd cut through the ravine after school and had lost a shoe in the mud. Kids talked about him sometimes, made a joke in the hallway or at the back of a classroom. He was known for doing stupid things.

Nabila didn't like hearing people talk about Matthew. She hadn't said a word to him in years, but she thought that people should know better, that he was probably still too delicate to be made fun of. There was something different about him: it was as if he believed everything, as if he couldn't always figure out when people weren't telling the truth. She'd heard guys say ridiculous things around him, making sure he'd hear, and then later they'd ask him what he thought about it. He'd repeat whatever they'd said.

That was the other thing about Matthew: he hadn't been able to tell when people were laughing at him. He always seemed to think that he was in on the joke too, and would smile along, and it infuriated Nabila. That was something he should have learned, she'd always thought. Something he should have defended against.

At the end of high school she'd gone to a party and Matthew had been there. He'd often been invited to things, she knew, but it was because he made a fool of himself, because people told him to do something dumb and he'd do it. Nabila hardly ever went out, she spent most of her time studying, but it was the end of grade twelve and the entire graduating class had been invited. She'd stood in the corner of the kitchen and had her first beer, and it had felt strange having so many people around, having the music and voices all be so loud. Then there had been a commotion in the living room, and everyone had run over, and there was Matthew lying on the ground, a cut stretching down his forearm. He'd been trying to walk along the mantelpiece, someone had explained.

Matthew was bleeding, and a girl handed him a piece of paper towel. Then she got more and wiped up the drops of blood on the hardwood. People were standing around in a circle, but they were drinking, talking, and Nabila realized then that no one was going to help Matthew up. They'd lost interest. He sat himself up, cradled his arm.

Nabila hadn't been able to bear it. She'd come up beside him to see if he was okay, helped him sit up against the sofa. She wet a few napkins and started cleaning off his arm. He didn't say much, just yes, he was fine, and then ouch, and it was the first time they'd talked since childhood. She wiped off the blood and he kept glancing at her face.

"You shouldn't listen when they tell you to do something," she'd told him.

He'd nodded.

He was really drunk and kept slouching over. Nabila righted him and propped him up with a pillow, then brought him a glass of water. "The ocean is rising, isn't it?" he'd mumbled, looking at her. "The ocean is rising and we should get to the top of a building."

"You remember," she'd said.

"I remember how cars are heating up the earth," he'd continued. His voice slurred a bit. "You always thought I wouldn't remember, but I did."

"You did."

The beer had made her head buzz, and it had made things seem softer, and suddenly a thought lodged itself in her drunk brain that she knew would never leave. It resonated back and forth, taking up space. There were so many things in the world that she couldn't save, seagulls trapped in oil spills, walruses with those plastic soda-can holders caught around their necks. So many things were out of her reach. But here was Matthew, right in front of her, his chin with the beginnings of a beard but his eyes still wide and unsure. He looked at her and it was as if they were back in the garden, just the two of them trying to survive.

Nabila patted his arm. On her own she couldn't save much, she understood, but maybe she could save him. Maybe she could help.

She sat with him for an hour, maybe more. A few guys came by and tried to get Matthew to go with them into the backyard, but Nabila told them to go away, to leave Matthew alone. They left and told everyone she was making out with him. Nabila didn't care. She got him a bottle of water, woke him up enough to take a few sips.

Every once in a while Matthew would raise his head, look for her.

"You shouldn't trust so many people," she told him one time. She shook his shoulder to make sure he was listening. "Matthew? Those guys aren't your friends. Okay?"

He nodded, but his eyes had closed. Nabila sighed.

Eventually she tried to get Matthew to stand up, but then he fell over, so she settled him on the couch. She brought him some chips, and he ate, then slept, and it started to get late.

Nabila's dad called to say he was picking her up, and she didn't know what to do. She couldn't leave Matthew there. But she didn't want to ask her dad to drive him home because he'd think they were together, she realized, and the thought of that mortified her. So she made a couple of friends give him a ride. She helped get him into the back of their car and watched as they drove off, feeling like she was somehow neglecting him. Even though she knew he wasn't her responsibility, a kind of obligation had somehow crept inside her. Nabila couldn't shake it off.

She didn't talk to him much after that night either, but the difference was that she'd started to feel guilty for not talking to him. She wondered if things would have been better for Matthew if she'd helped him sooner: if they'd been friends in elementary school, maybe he would have gotten to know more people, maybe he wouldn't now have to scrounge for friends who really just wanted to make fun of him.

Nabila saw him a bit that summer, walking down the street or in the grocery store. They'd wave and say hi, but that was it. Sometimes she wanted to ask how he was doing, but it seemed strange, so she never did. She noticed the cut on his arm had left a scar.

Then she started university, and her world had become biology textbooks and weekends spent in basement laboratories. There were suddenly so many new things that she wanted to think about. Her world became water, became the ocean and all the plants and animals that had to change themselves when it started to get warmer. It was fascinating, consuming. She spent entire days observing tanks of seaweed, learning how the plants grew, how they functioned. She loved the bright rooms that smelled of saltwater, the smooth, slimy feel of the plants when she brought them into air. She'd get up early and check on her specimens before heading to breakfast.

She'd worked on as many experiments as she could, assisting professors and grad students, taking long weekends to go and do fieldwork. Within a couple of years she was running her own projects, and by the time she'd started graduate school, she was scheduled to speak at her first conference. Colleagues asked for her opinions. People wanted to hear her ideas. In the last six months she'd been flown out to the Atlantic and Pacific coasts to study shore samples and to meet with faculty at other schools. She was focused on ocean warming, on how the change was affecting seaweeds. She wanted to compare samples from all along the Canadian coastline.

She hadn't thought much of Matthew through those years. She'd wondered about him, sometimes, wondered whether he'd gone to college, whether he'd moved out of his mother's place and had his own small apartment. She pictured him happier, taller, though she realized he probably hadn't grown since graduation. But she'd hoped he'd found his way.

And then there'd been that day when she stopped for French fries. She'd been away from the university, coming back from freshwater trials along Lake Huron. The restaurant had been on the outskirts of the city, along a street filled with strip malls. It actually hadn't been much of a restaurant. There was a storefront but inside it was just a counter for ordering, a few chairs to rest your bag while you waited.

She'd pulled over because French fries were easy to eat in the car. She'd gone inside, ordered from the girl by the cash register, then was standing there waiting when he'd appeared.

"Nabila?"

She hadn't recognized his voice. She turned around, and there was Matthew, coming around from the other side of the counter, a paper bag with grease stains in his right hand. He'd been wearing a white apron that had smears of ketchup across the front, had on a hairnet that exposed every corner of his face. The skin that was usually hidden beneath his hairline looked like chalk.

"Nabila. Hey. Wow."

"Hi Matthew."

"I can't believe it."

She'd laughed a bit, because it had seemed incredible, but also because Matthew had been watching her with such intensity that she'd felt uncomfortable. She'd turned to face him, and then he'd finally broken his stare, had smiled, said it was so good to see her. He'd said he'd get her a milkshake to go with the French fries.

He'd gone back behind the counter, started scooping ice cream into a cup, and she remembered thinking it was strange he hadn't asked her which flavour. He'd just chosen chocolate. He'd asked her about her work though, and she'd told him about the seaweed, and all he did was nod as he mixed the milkshake, sometimes glance up at her. He still seemed delicate. He looked a bit nervous, and she'd thought about the night of the party, wondered if he'd remembered any of it.

"How long have you worked here?" she'd asked him, and he'd been vague about the answer, said it had been a while and there'd been another restaurant before that. She'd asked if he lived nearby. He'd hesitated, but then said he still lived with his mother, but the commute wasn't too bad, that he'd made friends on the buses.

Nabila had hoped he would have done better. But she was also having trouble figuring him out. He still had a shyness about him, a way of looking that asked for approval, but there was something else beneath it now. It was the intensity that he'd watched her with at the beginning, a kind of focus. Maybe that was him now an adult, she'd thought. That was how his uncertainty had manifested. But she hadn't liked it; it had made her uneasy.

He'd been putting the lid on the milkshake when he'd asked for her number. He worked a lot, he said, hadn't been able to stay in touch with most people, but he'd like to stay in touch with her.

"Oh," she'd said. The uneasiness was making her hesitate.

He'd looked down, had looked hurt.

And then all her feelings from that party came rushing back, the guilt and neglect washing over her and trapping her in place.

"Do you have a pen?"

It didn't look like things had gotten any better for him since high school, Nabila thought, and if she could help him in some way, help him figure things out, she knew she should. Anyway, it was just a phone number. And it was the boy she used to share a forest with.

He'd watched her as she wrote the number on the back of an old receipt, and his hair was still so pale, she'd thought, his eyebrows blending right into his forehead. She'd handed him the piece of paper and he'd looked relieved.

She'd left then, and he'd walked her out the door, had stood waving on the pavement as she pulled away. She'd eaten her French fries and then drank the milkshake as she'd driven back into the city. The fries had been good, she remembered thinking, and so was the milkshake. It was thick and creamy. She would have preferred strawberry, though.

Nabila's parents get her a book for her eighth birthday, and she starts to dream about it. In the story, all the water disappears from the ocean, and people can walk on the ocean floor. They step over rocks and seaweed, walk up and down ocean mountains, jump across trenches. There are scuttling crabs, and dead fish and whales just laying there like roadkill.

Sometimes in Nabila's dreams though, the animals don't know the water is gone. They keep on swimming through the air as if everything is fine, and Nabila walks past them, watching them move as if still underwater. She walks through tall forests of kelp, and it sways slowly, pushed by an invisible current.

"Is it water that makes an ocean an ocean?" she asks her mother, wondering what she should call her dreamscape.

"It has to be saltwater," her mother says.

That makes Nabila think that her dreamscape is something else. She calls it a mind ocean. It is where her mind makes up the saltwater.

She thinks that explaining her mind ocean might help Matthew understand the forest game, but it just makes him more confused. They sit behind the bushes in the rooftop garden and she makes him close his eyes and try to create a mind forest on top of the building. Eventually he says he doesn't really want to do it, which doesn't bother Nabila as much as the fact that he doesn't have any better suggestions. "If you don't want to do something, you have to have another idea," she says, but he just stares at her.

Nabila wants to get mad, but she knows that Matthew can't stay long that day anyway. Her parents are coming home early because it is Nabila's grandmother's birthday. Her grandmother is dead, but they always celebrate anyway. Every year they go out for dinner, usually to the Mandarin, because they all like to eat chicken fried rice. Nabila tells Matthew about it and calls it a family tradition.

As soon as she finishes talking, Matthew says that he has a family tradition, too. When his father finishes his tour of duty, he will take them all to Canada's Wonderland to ride the rollercoasters. He will buy them cotton candy and win Matthew one of those giant stuffed bears at the whack-a-mole that he'll have to carry around with him all day.

"Really?" Nabila says when he stops, and raises her eyebrows. Matthew has never talked about his father like this before. It sounds to her like he is making it up. She just stares at him, and it is enough to make Matthew turn red. Then he won't look at her. He gets up and walks over to Samir and Tara Lynn who sit in the gazebo.

When Nabila comes out of the bushes, she finds Matthew hunched over in the shade, piling baby books in a tower while Samir watches and giggles. Then Samir sticks his fist out and they both shriek as the tower comes tumbling down. "I'm sure you won't knock it over this time," laughs Matthew as he pats Samir's head and starts building the tower all over again. Samir gurgles and tries to clap his hands together.

Nabila sits down with a thump beside Tara Lynn, who passes her the novel Nabila is studying in school. She takes it but she doesn't want to read. Instead she watches Matthew and her brother play as if the books were blocks.

When Tara Lynn stands up to talk to another woman on the other side of the gazebo, Nabila pokes Matthew's shoulder.

"Ouch," he says, still focused on the book tower.

"Don't worry, I won't tell anyone," Nabila says. "About your father."

"My father's a soldier," he says, sitting up straight.

"Right."

Neither of them say anything for a while after that. They listen to Tara Lynn talking with the other woman, to Samir squealing as the book blocks come down.

Then Matthew says, "You're lucky."

"Why?"

"You have a brother. I wish I had a brother."

Nabila snorts. "He's too little to be much fun."

"No he's not." Matthew ruffles Samir's hair again and the little boy smiles at him. "You play with him, right?"

Nabila shrugs. "Sometimes, I guess."

"You should play with him."

"Why do you care?"

"I don't know." Matthew wipes his nose on his sleeve. "He probably wants you to."

The book tower comes down again and Samir shrieks and bounces on his bum. Tara Lynn looks over, and Nabila realizes it's because she can't tell if he is laughing or crying.

When Tara Lynn comes back to the gazebo, Matthew is reading to Samir, and Samir is hanging on to Matthew's arm with his baby hands, a drop of drool pooling on his chin. Nabila sits away from them. She still wants to play the forest game, and she is thinking about using a flowerpot as a little basin where they can collect rain that they can use to water their seeds.

Matthew doesn't have a problem making things up in his mind, she realizes. He is good at that. He just doesn't see the forests and oceans that she can.

His sisters are late that day. When it gets close to dinnertime, Tara Lynn asks Matthew if it's okay if they walk him home. He says it's fine, that he has a key. That he is used to being home alone.

On the walk to his apartment, Matthew stays behind Nabila. He pushes Samir's stroller and chats with Tara Lynn, and Nabila walks ahead of everyone, scuffing the soles of her shoes against the sidewalk so that they make a slipping sound.

Tara Lynn asks Matthew what time his sisters will be home, and he says he isn't sure. Nabila looks out for them anyway. She likes talking to them. Sometimes, when they come to pick Matthew up, he takes a long time getting out of the elevator and hangs back with Samir and Tara Lynn. Then Nabila goes ahead of them to see his sisters, and ask them questions like what their favourite song is or if they have boyfriends.

They are twins and their names are Libby and Roxanne, but Nabila can never remember which one is which. She just knows that she likes the one with the pink hair the best.

Nabila wishes she had sisters, which is, she realizes, probably the same way Matthew felt when he said that he wants a brother. Libby and Roxanne chew gum all the time and pop bubbles in the middle of conversations. They wear plastic chokers that, from far away, look like tattoos.

When they drop Matthew off at his apartment building, Tara Lynn wants to walk him upstairs, but he insists they stay in the lobby. He takes out a key that attaches to a blue elastic band, the kind that holds stalks of broccoli together, and says he'd be fine from there. Nabila is disappointed because she wants to see what Libby and Roxanne's rooms look like.

Before Matthew leaves, he reaches into the stroller and pats Samir's hair, and Samir reaches up and grabs Matthew's finger and won't let go. "He's got a grip like a soldier," says Matthew.

Both Nabila and Tara Lynn laugh. Samir looks up at him, and, with the other hand, touches Matthew's cheek.

Tierney was already downstairs by the time Nabila awoke. She could hear her moving around in the kitchen, stacking dishes and singing along to the Glass Animals. There were cars driving along the street outside, a cool breeze coming through the window she'd left open. It made her sneeze.

She'd only left Canada a few times in her life. Once when she was too young to remember, when her parents had taken her on a trip to Pakistan, and then when she was in school they'd gone to Britain and the United States a couple of times. The States looked like Canada, she remembered, but Europe had different toilets, different light switches. The markings on the crosswalks were always strange. She was reminded of those differences now when she walked toward the door of her room, turned on the light.

Everything became bright and hurt her eyes. She kept going into the hallway, where the floor felt rough under her feet. The air smelled like wood. She went back into the bedroom and put her socks on, then shuffled along to the bathroom and washed her face. Her mouth tasted stale. She wasn't sure if she was just tired, or maybe a bit hungover.

She thought about calling her mother just to have someone to talk to, but then she'd have to explain everything. She'd rather not have to get into it all.

Her parents had never met Matthew, but she remembered talking to them at the dinner table as a kid, telling them how she and Matthew had made food or built a shelter, how they hid from airplanes and the news helicopters by ducking behind the rose bushes. But she'd always left out the details of their forest, of the fact that they were alone, surrounded by water. She knew that most of it should be kept secret between her and

Matthew. She remembered her mother asking about Matthew's family, and she told her about Libby and Roxanne, about how she wished that she had sisters. Her mother had said that Samir would grow up soon.

Nabila brushed her teeth and showered, and then realized she'd forgotten her towel in the bedroom again. She dried herself with her t-shirt and then put it back on along with her pyjama pants. The clothes stuck to her damp skin.

She wasn't entirely sure if she'd made the right decision. But she was here in Berlin now. She had to make it work.

She got dressed, twisted her wet hair up in a bun on the top of her head and secured it with a clip. There was lotion sitting on the dresser, and she rubbed some onto her hands and face, then dabbed her lashes with a bit of mascara. Matthew hadn't texted yet, and there was a bubble of anxiety in her chest about what might be happening. But she pushed it back down, told herself that she couldn't worry yet. She figured she should distract herself and go out today. There was an entire city for her to explore, and it would be better to go do something rather than just sit around all day waiting for him.

She ended up in Mauerpark, where there was a wall that ran around a soccer stadium, covered in pictures, in larger-than-life images of animals and rappers and buildings. There was a group of teenagers standing around with cans of spray paint, and one of them was up against the wall finishing the ears on a pink cat. Nabila walked past them and noticed that there was also a red-eyed wolf, a blue octopus with arms that stretched out in all directions.

Tierney had sent Nabila off into the park that morning, had told her that she had to see it because she could walk along the line of no man's land. It was where the wall had divided the east and west parts of the city, she'd explained, where people had jumped out of apartment windows trying to get to the other side, near the gate where women had smuggled across good cigarettes on visiting days by tucking them into their garters. Nabila walked through the park and then along the metal rods that marked the place of the wall. She peered through the rods and saw children playing on the other side.

Before Nabila had left for the day, she and Tierney had drunk lattes with brown sugar. Tierney had been waiting for customers and wanted to help Nabila decide what she should see first. She'd spread a sun-bleached map over the counter of the espresso bar and had traced the river as it wound through the city, curved around the island of museums. "If you had more time I'd take you canoeing down the Spree," she'd said.

If it had been another trip, another time, Nabila would have loved to see the river system. But she wasn't sure what was happening with Matthew and the longer she was away, the more could go wrong with her work back in Toronto. If her undergrad missed something, if her trials were ruined, things would be set back by weeks and she wouldn't be able to do her fieldwork in the spring. She hated waiting around for Matthew. She just needed to go out and think about something else until he texted.

"Keep your evening free," Tierney had said before Nabila left, and told her that they'd go together to Märchenwald, the Fairytale Forest, just on the edge of the city. It was worth seeing, Tierney said, because it was an old children's amusement park, but it had been abandoned and everything was now overgrown. Nabila could spend her days doing the tourist sites, Tierney had said, but the real highlight of her trip would be getting to know the other side of Berlin.

Nabila had said yes, mainly because she had nothing planned, and she didn't know anyone else in the city. But she also wondered about the overgrown park. It sounded like something she would have dreamed up as a kid.

She liked that about Berlin. She'd heard there were lots of places where nature had taken over human-made environments, and it seemed strangely magical to her, like her childhood games had actually been rooted in reality. In Berlin, trees could grow up through piles of rubble left over from the war, or through train tracks made obsolete by the old wall. Abandoned buildings became indoor gardens. Nabila imagined branches stretching up a staircase, vines hanging from old chandeliers.

Nabila walked around Mauerpark. There weren't many people out and she and wished she had someone to talk to, or even a conversation that she could eavesdrop on and understand. She felt disjointed, separated from the place around her. She could get Wi-Fi in a coffee shop, Tierney had said, but she had nothing really to say to anybody. And it was still too early in North America.

The night before, when she hadn't been able to fall asleep, she'd called her undergraduate and had seen that her kelp was all doing fine, that it was growing as expected and that everything had been documented with meticulous notes. The undergrad had been enthusiastic and wanted to tell her everything that had been done to make sure things ran smoothly in the lab. She sent her videos and even highlighted the cleanliness of the benches, how she'd replaced a light bulb at the back of the space that Nabila hadn't bothered with because it had been burnt out for months. Everything was running so smoothly. It gave Nabila a bit of a headache.

As she walked along the markers of the old wall, she thought about how easy it had been to step out of her life for a few days, to arrive in another part of the world with barely anything in her suitcase. She'd transplanted herself with hardly any effort. She'd only brought some clothes, a couple of books and the small package she had to give to Matthew. It was wrapped up tight in a small canvas bag, tucked in behind her toiletries. She'd checked again this morning to make sure it was still there.

Nabila walked until the wall memorial ended, then walked some more. There were big trees along the sidewalk, the cobblestones lifted in bumps where large roots were making their mark. She started to pass some newer buildings, glass and concrete, and then the cityscape changed and she noticed more tourists and souvenir shops. She stopped outside a café and checked her messages. There was nothing from Matthew. He'd given her a window of a few days, and she'd arrived at the start of it. There was still a lot of time. But if anything went wrong, if things didn't go as planned, she knew that he might need her help. Without any news though, all she could do was wait.

Nabila thought about sending her brother or her parents a note. She talked regularly with her mother about their research, but Nabila hadn't told her about reconnecting with Matthew. It was somehow like the forest game when she was a kid. Certain things, she didn't want to share.

She felt badly for not telling anybody that she was in Berlin, though she hadn't lied exactly, had just told them that she would be busy for a few days, that she'd call next week. That wasn't out of the ordinary for her anyway; she always worked long days when she was in the middle of a research project. She'd made friends with a couple of the other biologists at the lab and they teased each other about how much they all worked, were always the ones who were ready to fill in when other colleagues needed to go home to their kids. The three of them went out for drinks together at the end of most weeks; it was an evening out to fulfill their social quota, they joked. Those were Nabila's favourite days.

She bought herself a coffee and then walked through a square where there had once been a bonfire of books, then visited an art gallery and an old church where they were starting to set up the Christmas crèche. She sat in a field with fountains, and then noticed a plaque explaining how the area had been used for Nazi rallies. She passed through a long colonnade beside one of the museums, and realized the discoloured notches in the stone columns were actually bullet holes.

She felt superimposed upon a landscape that knew she didn't belong in. She wasn't sure the feeling would fade.

Nabila's brother, Samir, had told her about seeing Matthew at a gas station one night. It was a couple years ago now, and Samir was shocked that he'd recognized him, though Matthew didn't know who he was. It was a full-service station, and Samir was coming back from downtown in the early morning in a car with his friends. They'd pulled up to one of the pumps, and Matthew had come out to pump their gas.

It was summer, and they'd been at an all-ages club near the lakeshore, and Samir said most of them were pretty drunk. They started calling things out to Matthew as he stood there, just stupid things, like telling him he had a really shitty job but maybe he was too dumb to realize it. That maybe this was the best he could do.

Matthew had ignored them. That was when Samir said he realized that it was him, because of the way that he'd turned his head and then rubbed his ear as if he'd needed something to hold on to. He said he remembered seeing Matthew at Nabila's high school graduation, doing the same thing when his name was called. He said it made him look pathetic.

There was something about Matthew, Samir had told her then, that let the people around him realize they could take control. He didn't really want to join in on what his friends were doing, Samir said, but he didn't want to stop it, either, because Matthew had just made it all so easy.

They made him squeegee the windshield, Samir told her, and then one of his friends leaned out the car door, opened a water bottle and threw the water in his face.

Matthew has just stood there, shocked and sputtering, the squeegee still in his hand. The water made his shirt stick to his skin and he looked small, Samir said, and as if he didn't know what to do. Back in the car they had whooped and laughed, and then the driver had started the engine and they drove away without paying. Matthew was still standing there beneath the bright lights of the gas station, Samir said, watching them leave.

Nabila had been angry with her brother when he told her, and then she'd been angry with Matthew, because somehow he still hadn't learned. He still didn't understand.

When she saw him at the restaurant a few years later, she wanted to apologize for the incident, but also knew that it would have been worse for Matthew to know that had been Samir. He used to adore Samir. She didn't want to ruin that.

After she'd given Matthew her number he'd waited only a few days before sending her a message. It had mostly been an apology: he'd been so surprised to see her, he'd said, that he was worried he hadn't made a very good impression. That he was glad she'd come into the restaurant. That hopefully she'd had a good drive back.

Nabila had been able to picture him writing it, hunched over his phone. She wondered if the intensity she'd felt that evening had been anxiety instead—Matthew's reaction when he couldn't anticipate someone's response, when he wasn't sure what she'd think of him. Maybe he was used to people treating him the way Samir and his friends had. Once she'd considered that, she'd felt a bit badly. It was like he was stuck in high school, trying to walk across a mantelpiece, trying to slide down a banister, because he'd thought it would open people up, make him worth being around. Maybe that's what the milkshake had been: he'd been worried she'd no longer like him.

She'd written back and said it had been good to see him, and then he'd asked if they could have coffee sometime. She figured that there was no harm in catching up. So she'd chosen a place close to the university's big library.

Matthew had seemed anxious at first, but then she'd realized that he'd felt out of place. He'd stared at the pictures on the walls, kept playing with his cup and saucer and the little piece of chocolate that rested on the side. He'd never talked much, and she found herself carrying the conversation. She'd told him about her research at the university, then asked about his mother and his sisters, how they'd been doing. He'd said that he didn't see them much. That they all had their own lives going, and that he only went home to sleep.

He had a new group of friends, he'd said, nobody from high school, and she thought that was a good thing. He'd relaxed when she'd said it, had let go of the tension in his face. She'd wanted to tell him that it was okay. That he didn't need to be so nervous.

He still remembered the rooftop garden, he'd told her quietly, and that had made her happy, and she'd told him that she sometimes still thought about their forest game, too. Then he'd said that her coming into the restaurant that day had been a sign. She didn't know what he'd meant. He said then that he didn't really know, either. Just that it had seemed significant.

He'd looked so earnest when he'd said it, his eyes wide and full, that the only thing she'd done was smile. But she'd wondered about what

Matthew wanted. She'd tried to play it down, had talked about how it was always good to reconnect with friends, how it had worked out well. Matthew had nodded vigorously, the way he used to when she'd say they had to gather leaves and petals because they were running out of food.

He'd texted her regularly after that, usually every couple of weeks. He didn't say much except that work was good, though sometimes boring. That he hoped she was doing well. Every message said almost the same thing.

She'd write back a few days later, trying to include something interesting about the ocean, or new research on climate change, and he'd respond with wow, and how he didn't know that. They went back and forth like this for a few months.

It was hard for her to articulate the dynamic they shared. To her, Matthew was barely a friend, and not an equal friend at that; he needed someone to talk to, so she responded, but she never got anything in return. Maybe he was lonely, she figured, because his notes never hinted at him wanting something more. But still she wasn't sure.

Then, a few months in, he'd written her a message that was different. He was thinking of moving away, he'd said, of doing something completely different. His friends thought it was a good idea. They wanted him to do it because they said it would be better for him. What did she think?

She didn't know what to do with that text. It had felt strange. His message had been so vague but sounded so important, as if he'd wanted her to tell him what to do without really knowing the consequences. It wasn't the kind of message she'd wanted: it had strayed into different territory, into giving her more significance than she thought she deserved. She didn't know what he'd been expecting from her. So she'd decided to wait a few days before responding.

But then Matthew had showed up at her lab. He'd been waiting outside the door the next morning, and she'd almost walked right past him until she recognized the slope of his shoulders. He'd looked so sad that she thought he might start to cry.

She hadn't wanted her colleagues to see him, so she'd brought him into the basement laboratory, sat him down on a stool. She'd had her very first batch of Pacific kelp growing in canisters along the wall, and he'd stared at them, and then at the krill, and then had noticed the posters depicting North American drainage basins above the sink. "It doesn't matter to you if I leave?" he'd asked her quietly, while looking at the jar of krill, and then she thought that maybe her instinct to worry had been right, and that she'd let this go on for too long. Maybe she'd encouraged it. She hadn't meant to, had just been trying to be friendly. She'd been touched by his memories of the garden, the fact that he still seemed to look up to her. But he'd been getting the wrong idea.

"Should it?" she'd said, and she'd meant it to sound harsh, to make him realize that there wasn't anything between them. He'd looked at her as if she'd just punched him in the stomach.

She'd continued with her work, with checking the oxygen valves, and Matthew had sat there watching her. "What should I do?" he'd said a couple of times, and she'd shrugged her shoulders, said she didn't know. That she needed to focus on her research.

Eventually he'd gotten up. Even then he'd looked at her, as if expecting some final advice, some last-minute instruction. But she hadn't said anything.

"I'm supposed to leave," he'd whispered.

"Okay."

He walked out of the lab then, his eyes on his shoes, and closed the door. She'd told herself that it was necessary, that there was no other way. She'd needed to make sure that she didn't make things more complicated.

He'd relied on her too much, Nabila knew. He'd given her the kind of trust that she didn't deserve. But there was a part of her that had felt uneasy, even then, because Matthew had always trusted too many people. Almost everyone he met. And not many of them, she knew, would actually care about protecting him.

Nabila tells Matthew about octopuses. Her mother brought home a video where biologists put an octopus in a maze to see if it could find its way out. She tells Matthew about how it felt the space with its tentacles, trying to find an opening. Then it slowly worked its way through the maze until it got out. When the biologists picked it up and dropped it back in, it rushed through straight to the end. Octopuses have amazing memories, Nabila tells him. And they adapt to new things quickly.

When Matthew doesn't say much, Nabila tells him about other things that she thinks are fascinating. "If they're in trouble, they can even change the way they look," she says. "If they're in a rocky area, they can look like a rock, or if they're in coral, they can go all orange and yellow. It's true. They can change the colour of their skin. They can blend in anywhere."

They sit in the garden, behind the hedge, and Matthew tilts his head back, trying to balance a pebble on his nose.

"It's more than just the colour," Nabila says. "It's like they can change the texture, make their skin look rough. Or soft, or bumpy with little dots. Divers pass by them on the ocean floor and think they're just sand."

Matthew looks up at her, and the pebble falls, bouncing on his leg and then landing in the dirt. He leaves it there. "What if he has nothing to look like?" he says.

"What?"

"What if he's just on his own in the water? I mean, because if he sees rocks, he knows he's supposed to look like rocks. But if he doesn't see anything around, what's he supposed to look like?"

Nabila thinks for a moment. "Maybe it could change to look like the water."

"But water doesn't have a colour."

She shrugs. "It could make itself kind of clear or bluish or something. Or maybe it just stays how it started."

Matthew watches her carefully, his mouth slightly open. He looks down at the pebble, then looks back up at her again. He squints.

"I'm going to bring the video into class. Mom said I could. And Ms. Morrison said we'll watch it for science."

Matthew drops his head. "We don't get to watch movies."

"Ms. Morrison is the best," Nabila says. She pushes some dirt into a small pile, deciding she will make a kind of casserole for their dinner. She pats it down, adds more dirt. "Ms. Morrison is really nice. Have you seen her? She's really pretty, too. And every summer she travels to a different place in the world and takes pictures that she puts on the wall behind her desk. This year she's going to Cambodia. She's going to see this old temple that's been taken over by giant trees."

Matthew's mouth hangs open. "How giant?"

"They grow on the top and their roots go all the way down the side of the building to the ground. My dad's been there, too. He said he'll take me someday."

Matthew picks a bit of dirt from beneath his fingernail. "I wish we got to watch movies."

"It's a video to learn, Matthew. It's about biology." She sits up on her knees, pulls more dirt toward her. "Besides, your teacher lets you do all kinds of stuff. Doesn't she let you eat snacks during reading?"

"Sometimes."

"That's pretty nice."

"I guess." Matthew picks the pebble back up, balances it on the back of his hand. He stretches his fingers out wide. "I think she likes the girls in my class more though."

"Why?"

"She's always putting the boys in time out."

Nabila laughs. "Sounds like the boys don't listen," she says. There's a bit of dirt on her wrist, so she rolls up her shirt sleeves. "It's not that she likes the girls more. It's that the boys misbehave."

Matthew shifts his hand around, continues to stare at the pebble. "Still," he says. "I wish we had a man teacher."

"Why?"

He shrugs.

"There's only one man teacher in the school. And he teaches grade five."

"I wish he taught grade three."

Nabila rolls her eyes. She goes back to focusing on their shelter, gathering up sticks and leaves to make a barrier from the wind. She imagines an octopus moving along the flooded streets, becoming like concrete on the side of a building. She knows they can even adapt their skin to things that aren't in their natural habitat.

After a while, Matthew says, "How can they change the colour of their skin?"

"You mean what happens in their body? The science?"

"I guess. But no. More like how do they know."

"Know what?"

"Know what they're supposed to look like."

"They just do."

"But how?"

Nabila rests both of her hands on the ground. She pictures an octopus, its head like a full-to-bursting water balloon, its legs pushing through the water as if it is walking on clouds. She looks at Matthew. "I think it's one of those things that they can sense. Sometimes nature just knows things. Then they make themselves look like what they're around without even thinking."

Matthew frowns and drops the pebble again. He picks it up and holds it in both hands as if it is a warm egg.

"Animals just know some things. Like an octopus also knows exactly how big it is. Most animals don't know that. But an octopus knows exactly how big or small a space it can fit into."

Matthew stares down at the pebble. Nabila thinks about the maze, about how the octopus can squeeze its body into any shape because it has no bones. It only has a beak. That was the one part of the video that

Nabila didn't like. The biologists put the octopus in a box with only one hole, and the octopus tried to figure out the size. It felt the hole with one tentacle, then two more, moving them all around the edges. The hole is smaller than its beak, the biologist on the video explained, and its beak is the only part of its body that can't be squeezed. Nabila watched as the octopus realized this, and pulled back its tentacles. Then it just sat in the corner of the box.

That scared Nabila. To see it just give up. To know how smart it was, and then see that it couldn't do anything.

"Want to hear something else?" Nabila says. She lifts her hands out of the dirt, turns to Matthew. "After it lays eggs, the mother octopus has to stay close by and protect them. For a long time. It doesn't even leave to find food. By the time the eggs are ready, the mother octopus dies of starvation."

"Why?"

"I just told you. Because she doesn't leave her eggs to find food."

Matthew closes one hand over the pebble and holds it gently in his lap. He frowns. "The father octopus should go get food," he says.

"Only the mothers take care of the eggs."

"Why?"

"It's like that with a lot of animals. Humans are different from a lot of animals."

Matthew keeps his eyes fixed on his hands, and then Nabila realizes that maybe she shouldn't have said that. His face twitches a bit. She digs under the rose bush, finds a couple other pebbles that they buried earlier. She drops them in the dirt in front of him, and Matthew quietly picks them up, adds them to the one in his hand.

The water in the streets around their building is rising, Nabila thinks. She piles more sticks onto their shelter, adds more leaves. It is getting higher and deeper every day, consuming all the bottom floors, and she knows that soon they'll have to think about where they'll go next.

It was raining, Matthew remembered, the day he first met AJ. He'd been sitting in a window seat on the bus, watching droplets of water slide down the glass, collecting on the bottom. He was on his way to work and had been wondering if he should buy a raincoat. It was one of those things he never thought he really needed, Matthew had been thinking, but then days like this made him wish he were smarter.

That was when AJ had gotten on and slid into the seat next to him. He was wearing a rain jacket with a small hole in the sleeve, and water was dripping onto the floor. A few drops fell onto Matthew's pant leg, and he remembers how they turned small patches of his jeans dark blue, almost black. The seats were small and AJ's leg had pressed a bit against his.

Matthew wasn't used to having someone next to him. It wasn't a busy bus route, and usually his ride to work was solitary, a bit lonely.

He noticed there were other open seats. And yet there they were, sitting so close Matthew could smell the coffee on this man's breath.

"It might be a shit day," the man said then, and his voice seemed too loud. Matthew kept looking out the window.

The man then held out his hand for a shake, and Matthew turned to look. A stranger on the bus had never held out their hand to him before. The gesture seemed out of place, much too forward. He didn't really know what to do.

The man seemed to understand. He looked back at Matthew, then smiled just a bit, dropped his fingers onto his knee.

"What's your name?" he said instead.

Matthew still didn't know what to do.

"I'm AJ," he said. He leaned back in his seat and stretched his legs out as far as they could go until they hit the back of the seats in front of them.

"Always a shit day when it's raining. You can't get nothing done. You can't think straight with water all over your face."

Matthew nodded. He glanced up at AJ and saw that he was watching him. His eyes were blue, his chin was smattered with patchy stubble. Matthew looked away.

"What do you do?"

Matthew opened his mouth to speak, but instead of speaking, he started coughing.

"I work construction," he went on, using his sleeve to wipe a bit of sweat off his forehead. "You know. We're tearing up a sidewalk right now. By the time I get home there's dust everywhere. Or mud, with all this shit rain today. If they even let us work." He bounced his fist off the meaty part of his thigh and then exhaled loudly. There was again the smell of coffee.

"I work in a burger shop," Matthew said.

"Do you get free burgers?"

"No."

"Huh."

The bus ran through a puddle and water splashed up against the window. Matthew jumped back. "It's just for now," he said. "I'm not going to work there forever. But Mom makes me pay rent now. So yeah."

AJ looked at him. He nodded. "I know what you mean," he said.

Matthew saved him a seat every day after that. Talking to AJ always made him a bit nervous, but the thing was that he liked having talked to AJ, how the memory of it made him feel the rest of the time. So it felt right to keep doing it.

AJ talked a lot. Mostly about his work and his ex-girlfriend, but sometimes he also talked about things like the price of housing or why there weren't enough jobs. Every man on his construction site had to give up shifts every week, he told Matthew, so that there'd be enough to go around. Otherwise a few of them would be let go. He said those words with a kind of anger that scared Matthew; it made him picture one man holding the wrists of another man dangling down a well, and then losing his grip.

Things were broken, AJ said, in a place where a young man couldn't get decent work. Where he couldn't afford his own apartment.

Matthew didn't know anyone else who thought about things like that. He certainly never had. It made him wonder about his own job. He'd always thought the burger place wasn't really that bad, that it was good, actually, because he was doing it on his own and his manager liked him. But now he started to wonder if he'd been missing out.

One day, AJ invited him for a beer after work.

Matthew was so nervous that he couldn't eat lunch. It was a good nervous, the feeling he used to get before he rode his favourite roller-coaster, like there was too much energy running around inside of him. He put pickles on burgers when people didn't want pickles, forgot to clean the fryer for the onion rings. By the end of the day there were patches of sweat all along his back.

In the tiny employee bathroom he wet his hands and slicked his hair back before he left. AJ had picked a place that was halfway home, so Matthew took the bus for a while and then got off and walked down a side street. He was a bit early, but when he opened the door he saw AJ already sitting at the bar, his heavy boots resting on the rung of the stool and his glass half empty. He nodded at Matthew, and Matthew came in and sat down next to him like it was the most natural thing in the world.

AJ ordered him a beer and got another for himself. The food was shit at this bar, AJ told him, but at least the beer was cheap, and Matthew nodded, took several long sips and felt them go straight to his head. He couldn't remember the last time he was out for beer with a friend. His sister and him smoked together sometimes, but he hadn't had a beer in a while. He took another long sip.

Things were better once he was sitting next to AJ. He was used to watching him in profile; the sharp angle of his nose, the bits of grey along his temples, the tendency to not look straight at Matthew when he was talking. Soon they were drinking another beer, and then another, and AJ could be funny, Matthew realized; AJ was telling him jokes to try and make him laugh.

Matthew was so happy he could almost cry. He'd never really thought of himself as lonely—he saw his co-workers every day, his mother—but now he realized that this was what other people were used to doing. This was what other people looked forward to.

After a couple more beers, AJ got serious again. I want to help you, he said, and the words hit Matthew somewhere in his chest. I want to help you because I know you can do more, because I can see that you're better than all of this. I don't think you know that, he said, and Matthew thought that was about right. He'd never really imagined much more for himself. He'd never expected someone like AJ to notice him.

They drank past the time when everyone else had gone home, until the bar finally turned the music off. Matthew's entire body was spinning. He walked into the door frame on the way out, but AJ didn't laugh at him. Instead he gave him a Kleenex for his bleeding nose and then called him a cab. He asked Matthew his address and paid the driver.

Then Matthew remembered being in the back seat and barrelling down the Gardiner Expressway, straight for the lights of the buildings and the CN Tower. Everything was glowing in the darkness and the glass of the window was cool against his hand.

It was like he was flying, he remembered thinking. Like he had just left behind a world of sadness for a brand new one of colour.

After the night at the bar, AJ invited him to join the group. He mentioned it casually on the bus one morning, said that they met once a week and that Matthew should come to the next session. It was a group of interesting men, AJ told him, everyone young, who talked about their ideas for the world. Things like how they were going to change it. He thought Matthew would be a good addition.

AJ had written the address on a piece of paper and handed it to Matthew. Matthew had stuck it in his pants pocket and kept putting his hand over it for the rest of the day, had needed to make sure it was still there.

The meeting was at somebody's apartment, in a part of the city that Matthew didn't know very well. He found his way there after work.

He saw laundry hanging from balconies, teenagers skateboarding and filming each other with their phones. The neighbourhood smelled like burnt meat, like someone had been barbecuing on an open grill and then had just forgotten. Breathing it in made him nauseous.

In the lobby of the apartment building he buzzed the number AJ had given him, and the door opened. He went up the elevator.

Matthew didn't get invited to many friends' places. He could feel the sweat gathering between his shoulder blades, at his lower back. He wiped his palms on the sides of his thighs. He tried to remember all the things he knew he could turn to for small talk: the heat wave, the Blue Jays, the new Marvel movie.

AJ answered the door. He smiled and let Matthew inside. Matthew took off his shoes.

There were already four or five men in the kitchen. They were standing around and there was a bowl of ketchup chips on the counter. AJ introduced them to Matthew, and said that he would be joining them from now on, and everyone kind of nodded in his direction. Matthew stood there for a moment. Then he took a handful of chips.

Soon things had gotten started. AJ was like a thunderstorm, Matthew realized, all power and loud voice and slapping men on the shoulder. Matthew could tell that everybody else was a regular. They all knew each other.

AJ pulled chairs out of another room and made everyone sit in a circle—so close, Matthew noticed, that they were able to reach out and touch each other's noses. He wasn't used to being so close to other people. He focused on their socks on the kitchen laminate.

Then everything had gotten quiet. Matthew looked up, and saw that everyone was watching him. AJ leaned in even closer. He asked why Matthew was angry.

Until that moment, Matthew hadn't realized that he was. He'd never thought of it as an option. He remembered his father being the angry one, and then his sisters, and he didn't like being around them when they were like that. But he'd never really thought about being on the other side.

AJ asked him the question again. Then he mentioned the burger place. The other men started shaking their heads when they heard that. Someone asked if he had to wear a hairnet, said how that must be humiliating.

Matthew hated the hairnets. They made his ears stick out, made his forehead seem too big and his eyes too small. They made him look stupid. His manager had told him the first day that wearing it wasn't optional, but now it somehow felt like he'd been tricked. He looked around at the other men and felt ashamed. He put his head in his hands.

And then AJ was standing right in front of him, pulling him to his feet. Everyone was getting up then, trying to talk to him, trying to say that it was a good thing that he was finally seeing things for what they were. He'd been stifled for years, someone told him; someone else was sure he'd only known people who held him back. Now AJ was saying that things would be different, and he was holding Matthew's head with both hands and looking him right in the eye. Now he would show all those people in his life how stupid they were, he said.

They'd all sat in that circle for a couple of hours, and AJ had talked about the importance of men having good work. Matthew found himself nodding along. He'd always wanted to be a Marine when he was younger; he wasn't sure why he let that go. One of the other men shared how he'd just quit his job as a gardener because he was going to demand better. Others congratulated him, punched him on the shoulder. AJ agreed he was on the way to much bigger things. That life was going to be very different for him from now on. Another man talked about how he no longer wanted to be disrespected, and Matthew had never thought about that before, about having a say in how other people treated him.

Matthew left the apartment that night full of rage and awe. He didn't quite understand how he'd gotten there, but he didn't want to question it, didn't want to think too much about it. It was like he'd been waiting all his life for AJ to find him. AJ seemed to understand him, and it was a bit scary, but also made Matthew feel like he was finally home.

It was like he'd had a shell growing around him his entire life, stopping him from seeing the real world, and now that shell had been split open. Matthew hadn't known that he deserved more from things. That he was just in a place where young men like him didn't get the good options.

The next day Matthew took the usual bus to work, and AJ smiled and punched Matthew on the shoulder and said that he'd known he was one of the group since the first time they'd met. Matthew had never felt happier.

His manager was in the store when he arrived, so he put on his hairnet. But as soon as she left, he threw it in the trash. Then he ran his hands through his hair. His co-worker looked at him but didn't say anything. Then Matthew stood by the cash register with his arms crossed and his hair rumpled in a dozen different directions.

M atthew never missed a meeting. He didn't talk much but he liked to listen, and the men always had interesting things to say. They talked about how their mothers had always been controlling, and Matthew thought about his own mother, about her need to know he was getting shifts and making money. They talked about how employers preferred to hire women, so men like them had to scrounge for whatever jobs were left.

Matthew felt like an idiot for not having known these things, but he didn't let that on, just nodded at what they were saying. They explained why he was stuck where he was: the society they were living in was broken, and if he wanted anything different, he'd have to do something about it.

One day, the man who'd quit his job as a gardener was no longer there. AJ made an announcement about how he was on his journey, and everybody started cheering. Some men shook their heads and said they were jealous, but AJ assured them that they would all have a chance, but they needed to show him that they were ready. That they were willing to do what it took.

The next day on the bus, Matthew asked him about it.

AJ looked carefully at Matthew for a long time, and then said that he wasn't sure if he was ready to understand.

Matthew promised him that he was.

AJ watched him carefully, and then finally said okay, that he would tell him because he trusted him. Because he was part of the group now, and that he should also have the same chance.

Matthew held his breath.

Even though there were only a couple of other people sitting at the back of the bus, AJ dropped his voice to just above a whisper. They both leaned toward each other.

There's a place, AJ told him, where they were remaking the world the way it should be. Where men like them were putting together their ideas and working it into a reality. It was like an oasis. The group member who'd left had gone to join them. They needed only the strongest there now, the men who could help build the new society. Others in the group would hopefully go too, AJ said, once they proved they were ready.

Matthew had too many questions. AJ wouldn't answer most of them. Things were kept secret until you proved your worth, AJ said, but he said it gently as if he knew that Matthew would.

He told Matthew that this place would be a chance to start over, if he wanted. It would let him live life the way he wanted to.

When Matthew got off the bus that day, he was suddenly overcome by his thoughts. He sat on the bench at the bus shelter and watched cars go by. He'd never imagined that things could be remade, that he could go somewhere new and just restart, become someone else. It made him realize how insignificant his life had become. He wouldn't let that continue though, he promised himself. He'd make sure that things from now on would be different so that AJ would see he was getting ready.

It was later that same day that Nabila walked into the restaurant. For a moment Matthew couldn't talk, he just watched her. She hadn't recognized him yet. And then he realized that she might not recognize him at all, which terrified him.

He said hi. Nabila looked at him for a moment, and he could see that she didn't know. His stomach dropped. But then her face changed.

She seemed happy to see him. He remembered he was wearing a hairnet because his boss was in the back, and he was so ashamed she was seeing him like that. He busied himself with getting her food.

She talked about her university job, and he nodded, watched her face as her mouth moved. Her eyes were dark and her lashes were long, and her ears stuck out a little bit from her head.

He thought about the rooftop of her building where there'd been the forest, where there'd been the water surrounding them, and then the two of them in the middle of it all making dinner and building shelter. He'd seen her for years after that, in the school hallways, walking home. Then there was that party where he was too drunk and maybe he'd dreamed she was saving him, that the oceans were rising and she was pulling him up from the ground.

He watched her face and noticed how her eyebrows moved when she talked, how small strands of hair fell across her temples. Her skin looked so soft and he wanted to touch her cheek.

He handed her the milkshake and she was about to leave, and suddenly he couldn't bear to never see her again.

Can I have your phone number? he said, and she froze, and his entire body felt like it would disintegrate.

But then she nodded. She handed him a piece of paper and smiled. Matthew watched her walk away, and it was as if things weren't really all that bad then, as if his job was something good and the world was kind and his life was working out the way it should.

They went for coffee and talked, and it was like the two of them alone again in the garden, the rest of the world having been flooded away.

It was hard to stop thinking about her after that. Matthew knew that AJ would be disappointed in him, because he could tell that AJ would hate Nabila. That going to the group's oasis would mean leaving her behind. And it was confusing because thinking about her made him feel better. So he separated things out: he thought about her in the mornings before work, sometimes wrote her a message, and then put her aside and started thinking about all the awful things in his life before he boarded the bus to the burger place. He fixated on his parents, about how he'd never seen them when he was a kid. About how his job was stifling him. About how women never went out with him because he didn't look like the men they were trained to want.

But even though he tried, things always ended up coming back to Nabila. When he thought about his parents, he remembered her family and how she talked about their dinners together. He thought about her job at the university, wondered how she'd ever gotten so smart. And he wondered what her mouth tasted like now, if she had a boyfriend and what she did with him.

Matthew still wanted to show AJ he was getting ready for the journey—he still wanted to go to the new world more than anything—but Nabila was complicating things. His decision no longer seemed straightforward.

One day he thought he saw her on the sidewalk after work. He followed her for a few blocks, watched her black ponytail bob behind her as she walked, but then she turned around and he realized it wasn't Nabila. Matthew was so disappointed. All he could do was just keep walking, his hands in his pockets and his thoughts consumed by how he was tied to her.

When he finally stopped, it was already late and he'd missed the start of the group meeting. But he didn't feel like going anyway. Instead, he went home.

On the bus the next morning, AJ told Matthew to meet him for a beer after work again. Matthew wanted to say no, but he wasn't busy, and then he felt ashamed for trying to avoid him. AJ, he reminded himself, was the only person who believed in him. He was the only person trying to help Matthew become better.

Sometimes it was just so hard to focus, though. Matthew tried to be a valuable part of the group, attended the meetings and listened to anyone who spoke, but sometimes he spent the time figuring out when he would next write to Nabila. Then he started wishing that AJ wouldn't sit with him on the bus. If Matthew didn't think about Nabila, all of AJ's ideas still made sense. But he got confused when he realized all those things applied to her.

AJ wanted to meet at the same bar they'd gone to the first time. Matthew had gotten ketchup on his arms that day at work, and even though he'd tried to wash them, they felt sticky as he walked through the door. AJ was standing next to the bar this time, a nearly empty pint in his hand. His pants were splattered with dried cement.

Drink, he'd told Matthew, buying him one pint and then another. Matthew was nervous and swallowed the beer in big gulps. On the other side of the bar, people were playing a game of darts.

Then AJ made them sit at a table in the corner. He bought them fresh drinks, slammed the glass down so hard that the beer spilled over Matthew's arm.

I'm disappointed in you, AJ told him then. He shook his head at the wooden floor, and Matthew felt all the noise around him quiet, fade until it was barely there. Beneath the table he gripped his knee with his fingers to keep from shaking.

I thought you were one of the special ones, AJ said. Like you really understand what's going on. I thought you wanted to see things differently.

But I do, Matthew said.

AJ took a long sip of beer. Then he laughed, his face mean, and Matthew was scared.

I think you're lying, he said. Where were you yesterday?

Matthew couldn't move.

AJ sat back in his seat. He drained his beer. Then he took Matthew's beer right out of his hand and had a sip.

What aren't you telling me? he said.

Matthew felt like he was about to cry. He blinked his eyes fast and looked down at the table.

We're not leaving until you tell me.

AJ drank Matthew's beer and Matthew didn't say anything. Other sounds from the bar were emerging; people laughing, the thwack of a landing dart. He thought of Nabila, of the way her earrings dangled when she talked. He wondered if she was eating dinner right now, or drinking wine, or still working and standing over test tubes in her science lab.

AJ leaned forward. Have you forgotten? His voice was softer. You deserve more than this. A lot more. He handed the beer back and Matthew took a sip.

There was nothing to tell, Matthew thought. Not really. He just hadn't felt like going to the meeting yesterday because he was thinking of Nabila. And it's not like he saw her often. He'd just sent Nabila a few texts, had coffee with her. But he knew it was what AJ was looking for.

And he couldn't lie to AJ. Matthew knew he had to say something. So he mentioned how he'd thought he'd seen Nabila yesterday. He told him how they'd been friends when they were kids, and how he'd met her again recently. How she'd always been nice to him, that she wasn't really like other women. And that AJ shouldn't worry about her.

AJ listened well. Then he got up, bought them another drink. Matthew felt better. He didn't like hiding things.

But when AJ sat down Matthew could tell things weren't okay. AJ's jaw was clenched, his eyebrows were pulled together in an extended frown. Sometimes we can't see the truth, he told Matthew, pushing a beer toward him, and then gently explained to him that women often act nice at first, but that it doesn't mean anything. That Nabila could turn around and cut him off tomorrow.

She wasn't like that, Matthew tried to say, but AJ looked at him then like he felt bad for Matthew. Then Matthew started to feel stupid.

This is why only a few men are able to make the journey, AJ told him then. Because it was hard. Because you had to be vigilant and careful of people who tried to trick you. He put a hand on Matthew's shoulder. You can still come back to the group though, he said. If you try. I don't want to leave you behind.

The words stunned Matthew. He realized that no one had ever seen him the way AJ saw him, that no one had ever thought he had potential. He felt important, and then he remembered Nabila's smile and felt confused, and then he was crying, swallowing back tears and beer in the same gulp. He didn't know what to do.

They drank until the bar closed again, and Matthew didn't remember the end of the night but he remembered AJ putting an arm around him as they left and saying that things were going to be okay, that making the journey to their new world might be the best thing for him now. Matthew remembered nodding. And then he remembered AJ's smile, his lips pulled back, his breath hot with stale alcohol.

The next morning, though, Matthew wasn't so sure. AJ didn't know Nabila, he reminded himself. There was a chance he could be wrong. And he wondered what she would think of him making the journey. So he wrote to Nabila and asked what she thought about it all, but by evening she still hadn't responded and then he'd started to feel untethered. He wasn't sure of anything anymore.

He lay awake all night wondering if AJ was right about her, and in the morning he couldn't stand it anymore. He went to her laboratory, the one she always talked about near the big library. It was still early, so he waited outside the locked door. She would be surprised to see him, he knew, but he was hoping she would also be happy.

Instead, Nabila looked annoyed. She led him into a room that smelled like fish and that had tanks of water and plants, and then she just kept doing things as if he hadn't been there at all. He brought up his trip then, and he imagined that she'd be shocked he was actually considering it. But she didn't seem to care. She walked around from one counter to another, checked a thermometer, and she didn't say anything. Then she shrugged her shoulders, mumbled that it was up to him to decide.

Matthew didn't know what to do. At first he thought that she was pretending, that maybe she was trying to be brave, but when she looked at him he saw that she looked tired of him. She wanted the conversation to end. So he got up, and she made no move to keep him there. Then he walked out the door.

He took the streetcar home to get ready for work, and it was there, in his seat by the window looking out at the buildings, that he started to feel angry. Maybe Nabila wasn't the person he'd thought she was. Maybe AJ had known better all along.

AJ talked a lot on the bus that day, and Matthew listened, made sure he showed AJ that he was paying attention. It suddenly felt like AJ was the only real thing left in his life that he could hold on to. It was like everything else was falling away fast, and he needed desperately to steady himself.

When he got to work that day, he realized how tired he was. He put on his hairnet, and it was as if the shame of it ran down his entire body, coating him, making people laugh.

So he took it off. His boss came by and told him to put it on, and then everything in him suddenly let loose. Matthew yelled at her. He wasn't used to yelling, but in that moment it just happened, and it felt so good. Then he saw the shock and fear in her eyes, and he realized that it was because of him, that things had flipped and that he had the control. He wasn't used to that feeling. He was mesmerized by the power of his own loud voice.

Matthew was fired then, but he didn't care. He threw down his apron and walked out and had never felt so tall. He thought about Nabila, sitting in her science lab that smelled of fish, and wished he could yell at her, too. He pictured her backing up against the wall, terrified.

That night at the meeting, he told AJ what had happened. AJ grinned, punched him on the shoulder and said that he shouldn't wait any longer. He'd give him a list of steps, AJ said, and all Matthew had to do was follow.

The sun was just starting to set when Nabila finally made her way back to her room. She was glad to come home to the café, to see the plants and the books and listen to Tierney talk about her customers. Her plan was to do a bit of reading, to sit on her bed and take her mind off Matthew, but Tierney wanted to hang out, and all Nabila had wanted to do all day was talk to someone.

So they put a closed sign on the door and ordered Thai food for dinner, then opened a bottle of wine and sat on the floor of the backroom next to the trunk of the war tree. They spread out tea towels as if it were a picnic. Tierney put on classical music and told Nabila stories, and they drank and ate green curry and fried rice.

Nabila wasn't used to drinking so much, but she liked the idea that she did things differently in another city. They made their way through a bottle, and then opened another one. She leaned against the trunk of the tree and examined the bark, noticed how the small gap between the tree and the floorboards was filled with a kind of foam insulation. She hoped it wasn't hurting the tree.

Tierney was talking about a woman who had come into the café and bought a stack of books about psychology, then had shared a story about one of her friends who was renovating an old house that might be haunted.

"He's been working on it for months and every time he sleeps there," she told Nabila, "he wakes up and at least one light has been turned on. And once in the middle of the night, there was violin music coming from the kitchen. Like it was really soft, but he swore he could hear music as if someone was playing an instrument right there."

Nabila chewed rice and didn't know what to say. She played with her chopsticks.

"I told him he should have gone into the kitchen to check it out, but he didn't. Can you believe that?" Tierney giggled a bit, took another bite of her food. "He just lay in bed because he thought it was better not to know."

"Doesn't that make it harder?"

"Right? I think so."

Tierney laughed as if she were perfectly happy. Nabila took a long drink of her wine. Matthew still hadn't messaged her.

"So the Fairytale Forest tonight!" Tierney said then. "If you're still game?"

"Oh, right. I guess so?"

"Awesome! You're gonna love it. It's crazy. We'll walk to the bridge first, then the S-Bahn. Then we can go out tomorrow night. You're here for another three days, right? When does your boyfriend get here?"

"Three days. Yup."

"So has he just been travelling for fun? How long have you two been together?"

"Oh, you know. A few months." Nabila looked down at her plate because she was worried she was turning red. She didn't think she was a very good liar. "His family didn't travel at all when he was a kid, so he wanted to see a bunch of places. That's why he took the time to come over to Europe."

"Cool," Tierney said.

"How about you?" Nabila said quickly, and Tierney launched into a discussion about this DJ that she was kind of seeing, but kind of not, who played in a bunch of different places in the city. It was hard to meet people because she didn't speak German very well, she said, and Nabila realized that maybe that was part of the reason Tierney was so friendly, because she just didn't have many people here. She was almost giddy with excitement tonight, Nabila saw. For a moment she felt bad for Tierney, but then she also appreciated it because it meant she had someone to take her mind off everything.

Halfway through the second bottle Tierney decided it was time to go. They poured the rest of the wine into paper coffee cups and walked to the bridge to wait for the train. It was dark already. The air felt kind of warm, but Nabila wondered if that was just the wine. Her cheeks were flushed and she was feeling lighter, more at ease. She accepted the cigarillo when Tierney passed it to her, could see the dark purple wine stain that Tierney's mouth had left on it. She was suddenly the happiest she'd been all day. She hadn't understood how lonely she'd been walking around the city, how anxious she was about seeing Matthew again, and now Tierney was taking all of that away.

When the train finally rounded the corner and came into view, Tierney stubbed out the cigarillo. They walked to the S-Bahn and got on a train headed to the far side of the city. Nabila stared at the map and Tierney pointed to where they were going, to the station where they would disembark.

"The owner ran out of money," Tierney explained as the train stopped and a few people got off, and they found two free seats. "He created this amazing park, and then it just went bankrupt. They shut it all down."

Nabila looked out the window while the world beyond the train turned from concrete streets to trees, while she sipped from her paper cup as if she were holding a cappuccino.

"It was cheaper just to leave everything in his park there, so he did, and now it's this place where you don't really know what you'll see." Tierney was speaking louder than she probably realized. "It was small, but there was still a bunch of stuff. I won't ruin it for you, girl," she said as she grinned, the diamond glimmering against her red-wine teeth. "You'll see soon enough for yourself."

After a while they got off in a suburban area. They threw out their empty coffee cups, then walked for a long time through quieter and quieter streets. Nabila tried to remember the turns they were taking, the names on the road signs. She'd charged her phone before they left, knew she could always check the map if she had to, but she still wanted to be able to place herself. It felt strange to not really know where she was going.

Ahead of her, Tierney was walking with confidence, navigating the early darkness. The streetlights had come on and there were insects buzzing above them. Nabila's head was heavy with the wine, and her tongue felt thick, but she was glad to be out. She pushed thoughts of Matthew away and admired the vegetation.

Many trees had turned yellow but they still had their leaves, and Nabila wondered if that was normal in this part of the world for so late in the season. She wondered about the soil too, about whether the dampness of the city's swamp stretched out to the woodlands.

Tierney led them out to where the houses ended and pointed to a path cut through the trees. "The Fairytale Forest park is just inside the woods," she said, taking her phone out of her pocket and turning on the flashlight. "It's close to the edge where things were cleared. Five minutes more. Maybe ten. Sound good?"

"Let's go."

Nabila took out her phone too, shone the light on the path ahead of them. They were in an isolated area, she was realizing, were about to head off into more isolation, into where they couldn't be easily seen. But she was feeling a bit reckless: she was angry at herself for thinking so much about Matthew, for not being able to enjoy herself because she was worried about him. It shouldn't concern her so much that he hadn't sent her a message in a few days, she thought, and yet it did, more than she wanted to admit. So she plunged through the bushes, determined to leave him behind. Her heavy footsteps sank into the soil.

Their lights only illuminated a few feet ahead of them: just dirt and sticks, the stray branches of trees. Every once in a while Nabila heard the sound of a car in the distance, a squirrel or a bird in the canopy above. The two of them walked in silence.

Soon the forest started getting thicker. There was more underbrush, and branches hit her shins and arms. There were pine trees and their needles poked her as she pushed through. She put her hands up to protect her face. "How much farther?" she called to Tierney, but it came out quieter than she'd expected, as if she were just making conversation.

"Almost there."

A forest floor, she knew, was one of the most fertile places you could ever find. A mere handful of soil contained more tiny organisms than there were people on the planet. The annual supply of decaying leaves and fallen trees constantly replenished it, provided an incredibly efficient fertilizer. If the climate was right, almost anything could grow.

"Up ahead. See it?"

Tierney had stopped and Nabila almost walked into her. She stared at the space ahead of them illuminated by the phone light.

"Is that a fence?"

"Yeah. It's just chain link, nothing special."

"We're not climbing a fence."

"We don't need to." Tierney shone the light down toward the left, and Nabila saw a hole cut through at the bottom. "Piece of cake."

Tierney dropped down to her hands and knees and flattened her belly against the ground. She wriggled through and was then on the other side, standing up, brushing dirt from her pants. Nabila was going to ask if they were breaking any laws, but then decided not to. She pushed herself onto the soil, breathed in the smell of earth. She felt the fence pull a bit at her jacket, at her jeans. Then she emerged.

Tierney reached a hand down to help her up. Nabila turned to look at her, but ended up just looking past her.

They were in a clearing with tall grass and bushes, a sun-faded sign with a picture of a fortune teller hunched over a crystal ball. Beyond that were tall, thick linden trees, and standing above them was a curve of glinting metal.

"Is that a Ferris wheel?"

Tierney giggled, bounced on the balls of her feet.

It was completely dark now but there was a full moon, and the light was reflecting off the top of the wheel like a sun. The wind blew, and they heard the metal groan. The whole Ferris wheel was rotating very slowly. There were still seats on it, and they swayed, shining light in every direction.

"I had no idea," Nabila whispered.

Tierney began walking, pulled on her arm.

They didn't need their phone flashlights with the moon shining in the clearing. They passed the fortune teller sign and found another sign in German, then almost tripped over the edge of a raised stone pathway, its sides covered in tall grass. They followed it beneath an overhang of trees. There was a booth to their right, the same picture of the fortune teller on the outside wall. This time the paint of her hair was chipped off to reveal the wood beneath.

"I think there's a clearing over there," Tierney said, pointing. "It might be the pond."

"How many times have you been here?"

"A few." She grinned.

They left the pathway and pushed past branches. Nabila was feeling light, was feeling a giddiness that was maybe the combination of the wine and the spectacle, of the evening spent in a place where the forest had taken over. She wondered what Matthew would have thought of it, if he would have been as breathless as she was. She wondered what the trees said to each other in this place.

Tierney had moved to Nabila's right, was pulling back branches carefully. "Take your time here," she said, looking for a moment over her shoulder.

"Why?"

Nabila pulled back yellow leaves and suddenly saw something that was not leaves. It was more like the shape of a head. She jumped back.

"You found one!"

Tierney yanked back the branch that Nabila had let go of and turned on her flashlight. It was the head of a swan, its long black beak almost stabbing them in the eye. Nabila caught her breath as she saw its painted features, realized that it was a statue almost the same size as her. "They're boats," Tierney explained, almost jumping with excitement. She stepped around to the side and knocked on the swan neck as if it were a door. "See? Hollow plastic. People used to ride in them."

"That's a boat?"

Nabila reached out a hand and touched the neck, discovered that it was cool and slimy with a layer of moss spores. She felt for the sides of the swan, then stepped inside, sat gingerly on the seat that was covered in small plants. Leaves crunched beneath her feet against the plastic bottom.

"So," Nabila said. "Which way's the water?"

Tierney helped her out of the swan and they started walking through the woods again. This must be a place where teenagers come, Nabila thought, where they tried to escape everything else, where they didn't know what to expect. They could crawl under a fence and drink vodka and look for things from storybooks, ignoring the rest of the world. It didn't surprise her that Tierney, despite her age, was still coming here.

"How illegal is this?" she asked.

"Not that illegal."

"What does that mean?"

Tierney shrugged, grinned again. She pulled a twig from her pony-tail. "People sneak in all the time. It's too fun."

The trees stopped abruptly. Nabila stepped out onto a sandbar, a short strip of pebbles and sand on the edge of a pond. The moon was bright against the water, rippling across the surface. Tierney pulled on her sleeve. "There's another one."

This swan was almost submerged, the white boat body glowing in the moonlight beneath the water, the top of the neck and head just above the surface as if it were trying to breathe. Nabila shuddered as she stared at it. The body glowed almost green, a kind of ghost. The water played tricks with the angles, made it look as if the neck was snapped.

They walked down the beach, their shoes sinking into the sand and leaving a trail behind them. It was strangely quiet, as if they were completely alone, Nabila thought, as if the fake birds had scared the real ones away. There were two more swan heads watching them from the nearby trees. A fifth boat was on the other side of the water, its tail pointed into the pond. When Nabila focused on it, she realized it was missing its head.

"Over there. By that root," Tierney said.

Nabila looked down and saw the black of the plastic beak lying on the sand. She bent toward the ground, gently put her hand over the swan eye. It unnerved her. Then she touched the place that should have attached to the rest of the neck and found it hollow.

"I have a friend who says he used to come here when he was a kid," Tierney told her as she led the way across the rest of the beach, back into the bushes. "His mom used to take him to ride the swan boats, and he said even then the place felt creepy. Like the forest was already starting to encroach. Like you thought the park should be a fairy tale but it didn't ever shape up quite right."

"It feels like that now."

"Just wait. You haven't seen anything yet."

Tierney grinned again, and Nabila smiled back, but there was something starting to lodge in the back of her mind, a twinge of uneasiness. It was more than just the broken swans: it was a feeling that things were going wrong, that she should know better than to be there. And she needed to pee.

Tierney walked along the side of the pond and then disappeared back into the trees. Nabila ran to catch up. They were back on a stone path but the vegetation was too thick to see where she was placing her feet, and for some reason she thought of Matthew at that high school party, too drunk to sit up straight but egged on by people to walk the mantel. Doing what they wanted him to do. She'd always known better than that, but now she was at the whim of Tierney, following wherever she wanted to go. And she couldn't leave. She wouldn't be able to find her way back.

"How long do you usually stay here?" Nabila asked.

"Until whenever. Look, see that? Up ahead."

The excursion was harmless, Nabila told herself. Tierney was maybe a bit reckless, but she was so friendly because she was so lonely. And Tierney had been here before and knew this place. Nabila took a deep breath, told herself to relax.

Then there was some noise in the background, a kind of squeaking. Nabila thought that maybe it was an animal at first, but then realized that it was more metallic than alive, that it must be the metal of the Ferris wheel. They were closer now, and it was louder.

Tierney had heard it too. She raised a finger to her lips, turned her ear to the sky.

"Let's go find it."

"Really? Shouldn't we leave soon?"

"Soon. After the Ferris wheel. It's not far, just past the pirate ship. Then we can continue walking to the fence. We've already made a bit of a loop, so we can just keep going and leave the way we came."

Nabila wanted to protest, but it sounded as if they had to head in that direction anyway. So she let Tierney guide them around the edge of the carousel, back into the trees, then out into another clearing. They saw a billboard advertising pink ice cream, the bottom part of the sign ripped and hanging off the edge. They stepped across stone tiles that were painted in different colours. Then they passed a few tall trees and walked down along the side of a shallow gully, which Nabila immediately recognized as a dry riverbed. The sides were too steep, which meant it had been artificially made. There were sprigs of weeds growing along the bottom.

"We're coming to the best part," Tierney was saying, and Nabila caught herself wondering if Tierney befriended all her guests, was in the habit of taking them to strange places in the middle of the night. "It's just up ahead. You'll see it in a second."

They turned a corner and there was suddenly a dark shape in front of them, looming in the middle of the riverbed. "It's a shipwreck," Nabila gasped, and saw how the hull fit the width of the river perfectly, how they'd been designed to go together. There was a mast leaning up against the bank, a flag trampled with mud that bore the skull and crossbones.

Beyond that though, something was glittering in the dark sky.

They'd found the Ferris wheel. It was tall and silver in the moonlight, stretching much higher than Nabila had thought it would. The seats that were still attached swayed slightly in the wind. The metal squeaked, the sound loud and disconcerting, and everything slowly rotated. There was another smaller chain-link fence around the base of the wheel, but Nabila could see right through it to the old ticket booth with its broken glass, with a branch that had fallen across its roof. Maple trees grew along the old boarding platform.

"Incredible," she whispered, and Tierney squealed, started running toward it.

"Tierney, wait up. Not so fast."

But Tierney didn't stop. She sprinted toward the fence.

"Tierney! What are you doing?"

Nabila tried to catch up. Ahead of her, Tierney was approaching the fence. She wasn't slowing down. When she got to it, she scaled it in a few movements and landed on the other side.

"You're not serious. Tierney? Tierney!"

"It's fun Nabila! Come on!"

Nabila stopped at the edge of the fence and peered through it. On the other side, Tierney was pushing leaves and branches out of the way as she climbed onto the old boarding platform.

"I'm not coming. You're not actually getting on there, right?"

Tierney turned around to look at Nabila, grinned again, then turned her face toward the stars and whooped. "Suit yourself!" she said, and then jumped into the nearest seat. The entire wheel shook. Nabila held her breath as the metal squeaked and groaned, but then it seemed to settle back into place. A breeze ruffled the leaves on the trees, and Tierney started to creep slowly upwards.

Tierney was a daredevil. Nabila wished she'd realized this before. She was hanging onto the rod attached to the seat, dangling her feet off the edge, a massive smile on her face. She was like a kid on a swing set.

Nabila could do nothing but watch. She held on to the fence, felt the pulse of her heartbeat in her fingers.

Tierney swivelled with her chair, looking out in all directions, taking in the starlight. The wheel moved slowly. She sat there quietly, and at first Nabila wondered if she was scared, if she was having second thoughts. But she was still smiling. Then Nabila realized that Tierney knew she was visible up there. There was probably security guarding the park, Nabila realized, maybe a patrol around the perimeter, a small team scanning the major areas. She felt stupid that she hadn't thought about that before. The thrill of the spectacle and the wine was wearing off now, and all Nabila wanted to do was leave.

She didn't know which way the hole in the fence was, though. She couldn't believe how careless she'd been, how ridiculous it now seemed that she'd trusted Tierney. Now she had to wait for Tierney to come down.

Nabila clenched her fingers around the metal of the fence and closed her eyes. She should have thought more about things. Not just about the Fairytale Forest, but Berlin in general, the fact that she came here in the first place. When she'd gotten her ticket, it had all seemed to make sense. It had seemed necessary. But now she wondered about her decisions.

She looked back up to see Tierney's progress, and was just in time to watch as her chair slowly moved into the top position on the wheel. It looked windier up there. Tierney's arms were now wrapped around the rod, and she'd pulled her legs in so they weren't hanging down. Her hair was whipping around her face. Nabila tried to figure out how high off the ground she was, but she couldn't quite gauge the distance. She just knew it was too far to safely fall from.

She'd never really thought about the height of the building when she and Matthew used to play the forest game, because it had somehow seemed irrelevant. The trees around them were the important part, and the water in the streets. Even these days, she was always looking down into water. She wasn't used to looking up.

The progress of the wheel seemed to take forever. It stopped completely a couple of times when the wind stilled and then Nabila held her breath, wondered what they would do if Tierney got stuck up there. But each time a breeze would eventually blow, and the metal would squeak, the turning would start up again. Tierney would shift to the left and to the right, throw her head back and look at the moon. Nabila stood there patiently.

It was when Tierney was almost back on the boarding platform, her feet almost touching down, when the barking started. Nabila hadn't been able to place the sound at first. She heard something in the distance, a noise that shouldn't have been there, and then saw Tierney turn her head as if listening. The sound got louder. It wasn't part of the forest, but it was an animal noise. That's when Nabila realized there were dogs.

Her mind started to race. Of course security for a park like this would use dogs; it was probably the only way they ever caught anybody. Unless intruders were brazen enough to ride the Ferris wheel, she thought. That would make it easier.

"Tierney? Tierney!" she hissed.

Tierney's feet were grazing the platform, and then she leapt onto the concrete. She landed and started running in the same stride. Then she jumped down into the trees, turned toward the fence where Nabila was waiting. In a moment she had scaled it and was on the other side.

"Time to go!" she said, pulling Nabila's arm.

"No kidding."

They took off running around the left side of the Ferris wheel, crashing through underbrush. The barking was still there in the background. It was incessant. Nabila wondered what kind of dogs they would use.

"Are you sure we're not heading toward them?" she said between breaths.

"I'm sure."

"How are you sure?"

"Because the guards always come from the south."

Nabila felt her face get hot. "Always? What do mean, always?"

"Just always. Look out, there's a swamp on the left. Stay behind me."

Nabila ran fast and dodged trees. Tierney had known the place was illegal to enter and that it was guarded, and she'd probably even known that they had dogs. She'd acted like the excursion was harmless. Now Nabila might get her ankles bitten and get arrested for breaking into an amusement park.

They ran without flashlights, and branches whipped Nabila's face and arms. She knew she had to keep Tierney in her sight, had to make sure she stayed just behind her. They passed a clearing and out of the corner of her eye she thought she saw statues, but she didn't turn to look. The dogs seemed to be getting louder.

She couldn't tell how long they ran for. There was a cut down her arm but it didn't hurt, a bunch of leaves stuck in the hood of her jacket that she didn't have time to remove. The right leg of Tierney's pants had a rip in them. The forest went on and on and she had no idea where she was or why she was there. She just kept moving. She ran and hoped that they would make it out.

And then there was suddenly moonlight again. They broke out of the dense trees and were in a field of grasses, and Nabila saw the sign for the fortune teller.

"Almost there," Tierney said, looking back over her shoulder to make sure Nabila was keeping up. "We just have to get past the fence. Then they can't prove anything."

The barking was close now. Nabila resisted the need to turn around, kept her eyes focused on the chain link at the end of the clearing. Tierney knew exactly where to go. She guided them to the right and there was the hole, and then she was down on the ground and wriggling herself through it.

She was barely out the other side when Nabila dropped to the earth herself, started crawling through the hole. The barking was so loud behind her. She pictured what she must look like on the ground, imagined dogs with white teeth coming up and biting her leg muscles. She used her elbows to push through the dirt. She scraped her chin. She hadn't really even wanted to come. It had just seemed like a decent idea.

And then she was past the fence.

Tierney helped her up onto her feet and the two of them started running again, through the beginnings of the forest, back out the way they came. The dogs kept barking, but the sound started to get farther away.

It was okay, Nabila tried to tell herself as they wove through the trees. It was over now. They'd made it out.

But Tierney kept running, so she did, too. They didn't stop until they hit the road.

It was supposed to feel like home, but they'd used the big trees for target practice and all Matthew could focus on were the bullet holes. Some rounds were still lodged inside the trunks. Others had just sliced off bits of bark, and Matthew realized the fields behind the trees must be filled with them.

Something about shooting made him want to vomit. He had finally arrived at the place he'd dreamed about, was finally meeting his new brothers, but all he could think about were the trees. Their wood was scarred, cut up and marked in ways it shouldn't have been. Most of them were still trying to grow leaves, but there were lots of dead branches, places where the wood had been snapped at unnatural angles.

He'd been travelling for almost two days. Once his plane had landed in Berlin, he'd turned on his phone and had gotten instructions from AJ about catching a city bus. He rode it until the last stop, which was on the outskirts of Berlin. Then he'd stood there on the sidewalk, waiting. He only had one duffle bag. Someone would come by to pick him up at that spot, AJ had told him. He might have to wait a bit, but he didn't need to worry, AJ said, because everything was taken care of.

Matthew tried to relax. When his legs got tired, he sat on his duffle. The air wasn't cold yet, it was the middle of the afternoon and his phone battery was still charged. He opened the can of Coke that he'd bought at the airport. It was warm and he drank it slowly, the bubbles pricking his throat.

He knew AJ would make sure things were okay. Matthew was just on the edge of the suburbs, could see a few houses up the street. He finished his Coke and then peed in the clump of bushes behind him.

It was nearly evening by the time the pickup arrived. It was white and rusting, and it rolled to a stop right in front of him on the side of the street. A man got out of the driver's side and Matthew stood up.

The man didn't shake Matthew's hand, just told him he could call him Tom and they were running late so he better get in. He grabbed Matthew's duffle and threw it in the back. Matthew got in the passenger's side and put on his seat belt. Tom started the truck and began driving.

He did most of the pickups, Tom told Matthew, at least all of the ones that came through Berlin. Sometimes people flew into Dresden instead, he said, and there were others that just drove out there by themselves. But the Berlin pickups were his domain. He slapped the steering wheel for effect.

There were takeout wrappers on the floor of the cab, a dark stain on the side of Matthew's seat and part of the door. They had left the suburbs now, were speeding down a highway with farmers' fields on both sides. He liked driving, Tom said, because he sometimes had time to stop at a strip club, and he got to meet the new recruits first and suss them out. Part of his job was quality control, he said. He looked over at Matthew, took one of his hands off the wheel to dramatically stroke his chin. "I know your type," he said. "You're scared." Tom then laughed. Matthew felt his stomach tighten.

Tom had been one of the first recruits, and he told Matthew how they got a steady stream of guns from Eastern Europe, hidden between other goods in big trucks. Target practice was an important part of life at headquarters. "Bet you never fired an automatic before," Tom said, then laughed again when Matthew looked away.

They'd driven for hours and Matthew had fallen asleep, his head resting on the window. He'd woken up to Tom shaking his arm because they'd arrived.

The trees used for target practice were at the back of headquarters, outlining a field where crops used to grow. Now there were just dead plants and dried soil, along with dozens, maybe hundreds, of stray bullets.

There were too many people to meet. Tom began shouting names and pointing to men, maybe fifteen or twenty in total. One of them was the general who ran the place. Matthew was supposed to report to him later. Then lots of other people were suddenly grabbing Matthew's hand, clapping him on the back. Someone had come from Australia, another from the United States, India and Russia. A bunch of them were from Poland or Germany. Everyone seemed to speak English, but Matthew heard lots of different accents. AJ had told him that the chance to train with the group in person was special, because most people only communicated online. Matthew tried to keep track of names but it was too difficult.

The sun was hot and he was sweating beneath his jacket. He was nervous, stuttered when they asked him his own name. His mouth was dry.

There was an old barn that they called the barracks. Matthew was led inside and saw sleeping bags, partitions of wooden boards and blankets that some of the men had put up to separate their space. He got a spot somewhere in the middle and left his duffle bag there. AJ had forgotten to tell him to pack a sleeping bag, but there were some extras.

Next to the barracks were two old farmhouses. One of them was the general's quarters, and the other was for food and supplies. In the second house they had two recruits working as chefs cooking in the kitchen, and everyone ate together at long tables in the unfinished basement called the mess hall. There were two bathrooms in the house, and you could have a shower every other day if you wanted one. You weren't supposed to use the indoor toilets: they were stuck shut, and there were two outhouses at the back of the property instead. There was also a wash station outside the barracks.

They told him there was a strict schedule. Everyone had to get up early to train, just like any army. They had a few acres of old farmland, and you had to run laps around the dead cornfields and then meet in front of the barracks for strength training. Then it was breakfast in the mess hall, then morning target practice. Matthew would get his gun soon. There was lunch after that, then more target practice, then group meetings like the ones he was used to, then dinner. They had the evenings off.

This was what Matthew wanted, what Matthew had chosen, and he tried to focus on that. He tried to stay calm, tried to remember why he'd come. But now that he was there, he had trouble finding his anger. He tried to remember what it felt like to yell, thought of Nabila, but in that moment, all of his rage had somehow fallen apart. He couldn't remember anyone's name, except for Tom's. He figured he should make conversation but he couldn't think of anything to say.

He went back to the barracks to set up his sleeping bag. There were a couple of men already standing in his space though. One of them was Tom. They had his duffle bag open and were pulling out the chocolate bars that he'd brought with him.

Tom grinned as he stood up, slapped Matthew's shoulder a bit too hard. Matthew just stared at him.

"Think of it as a contribution," Tom said, as he ripped open a wrapper. "A thank you for the drive." Then he laughed with the other man, walked out of the building.

Matthew stood there and watched them leave.

Matthew and Nabila never play together at school. In Nabila's class, she sits at the front with her friends, and she knows that in Matthew's classroom, he has a spot at the back next to the pencil sharpener. At recess she plays tag or jump rope, or even Red Rover if there is a group of them playing and the teachers aren't watching. Matthew likes to hang out by the soccer field, but he doesn't play that often. He mostly just sits on the sidelines and watches. If the ball comes toward him, sometimes he'll give it a kick, winding up first and setting his mouth in intense concentration.

The two of them never talk at school, don't look at each other if they pass in the hallway. They always stick to that, even though they never specifically say anything about it. Nabila likes that they can do that.

She always takes a long time getting her things together after school is over. She talks to her teacher, asks her questions about the pictures she has taped behind her desk from her travels, asks her what books they'll read next and if she can help choose one of their novel studies. She unpacks her backpack, then repacks it, making sure everything fits the way she wants it to. She goes to the bathroom and checks if the leaking tap on the far end is still leaking.

Only after that does she go outside and meet Tara Lynn, Samir and Matthew. By then, most of her classmates have already left, and there is nobody around to see them walking home together.

The day they get their report cards, Nabila and her friends stand in the hallway after class and compare grades. Most of them have a combination of As and some Bs, though Nabila has straight As. She is probably the smartest person in the class, her friends agree, and maybe even in all of grade three. Nabila feels like she is flying.

Nabila wants to see what grades Matthew got, but he won't show his report card to her. They walk home behind Tara Lynn and Samir, and Nabila keeps trying to get him to cave and open the envelope. When he still refuses, she takes out her own report card and starts reading out the letters. "An A in literacy, for comprehension and application," she says. "And then an A plus and another two As in math. A pleasure to teach. Look, that's what Ms. Morrison wrote. Right there. A pleasure to teach."

She shoves the paper in Matthew's face and he bats it away. He keeps his own orange envelope held firmly in front of him.

In the rooftop garden, Matthew sits on his envelope to make sure Nabila can't get at it. He pokes a stick in the dirt while she mixes together plants that escaped the rising sea levels. When Tara Lynn calls to him that his sisters are in the lobby, he grabs his envelope, now smudged with dirt, and takes off downstairs.

He leaves so quickly that he forgets his jacket. Nabila tells Tara Lynn that she'll go give it to him, and runs to catch the elevator.

"You forgot something!" she calls, just as Matthew and his sisters walk out the main doors. She comes up behind them and sticks Matthew's hood over his head so that it falls down and covers his eyes.

She looks at his sisters, who are both wearing coats so short that an inch of skin is still visible above their pants. "Did he show you his report card?" she asks. "He wouldn't let me see. I was just curious." She swats at the empty sleeve of Matthew's coat and he hides the envelope behind his back.

The pink-haired sister stretches her jacket sleeves down over her hands. "What's the big deal?" she says. "It's not like it really matters anyway."

Nabila feels her face get hot. "I showed him mine."

The other sister shrugs. "Then show her yours, Matt."

"I don't want to."

"Oh for Christ's sake," she says. She lunges at Matthew and snatches the envelope out of his hands.

"Give it back!" he cries. His jacket falls to the floor as he tries to grab the envelope, but his sister holds it above her head. Her coat rises up above her belly button and Nabila sees a piercing with a turquoise star. The sister slides her nail under the flap of the envelope and tears it open. The other sister takes out the report card.

"C minus, C minus and D in math," she reads. "Some more Cs in reading. Then a B minus in gym, hey, that's not too bad—"

"Stop it!" Matthew screams. He jumps up to try and get it but can only hit his sister's arm.

"What's wrong with you?" she says, and slaps his arm right back.

Nabila's stomach feels queasy. Other people in the lobby turn to look at them. Matthew's lip quivers, and his eyes look red and glassy like marbles. Both his sisters are looking at the page now, reading it in the air high above his head. They both snap purple bubble gum between their teeth. The one with blonde hair wears spaghetti straps under her half-open coat, and Nabila notices the corner of a leopard-print bra sticking out.

"He needs to focus more on homework," Matthew's sister says, tilting the paper toward her. "And actually learn how to write sentences, apparently." She looks up at Nabila. "Anything else you want to know?"

Nabila shakes her head.

His sisters stuff the paper back into the envelope, then toss it toward Matthew. He catches it and then wipes his eyes with the back of his hand.

"Don't be such a baby," the pink-haired sister says. "It's not a big deal."

"I'm telling Mom," he says.

"Sure. Go ahead and tell Mom. But her shift isn't over until midnight, when you'll probably be asleep. And she'll be more worried about your D in spelling."

The other sister looks over at Nabila and juts out her chin. "What did you get in spelling?"

"A," she says.

"Huh. Girls are smarter."

Matthew turns toward Nabila. She thinks he is going to say something, but after a moment he just looks away and focuses on his boots.

"Come on, let's go," his sister says. Both sisters turn and walk out of the lobby with their hands in their coat pockets. Matthew and Nabila are left standing there.

"I'm sorry," Nabila says quietly.

Matthew doesn't look at her. He just picks up his jacket and folds it over his arm, then holds onto his report card with the other hand. His sisters have already started making their way down the sidewalk, and Nabila watches him run to try and catch up to them.

Matthew woke up before it was light out. He heard someone snoring, and the call of a bird, maybe a crow, outside in the sky. He shifted in his sleeping bag and the floorboards creaked beneath him.

This would be his first full day with the group. His mouth was dry, and he wished he had something to drink, something to take the bad breath off his tongue. He was cold. He kept thinking about how many people were sleeping right around him, how close they were, and how they might stir if he moved.

The night before he'd shot his new gun for the first time. It had been dark by then, so he thought they would have waited, but it turns out that getting your gun is a bit of a ceremony on arrival. They all went to the shooting range where they had a couple of floodlights pointed toward the target trees. Everyone stood by while the general walked up to Matthew and handed him the biggest rifle he'd ever seen. Then they waited for him to shoot.

It was even heavier than Matthew had thought it would be, and his arm kept dropping, the muscles shaking. The first time he hoisted it back against his shoulder he was worried he'd let it go. He almost had. But then his finger twitched and the trigger went and there was an explosion like fireworks going off in his hands. He felt the force of it in his rib cage. The bullets flew past the trees, and then one of them hit, and the men around him shouted and cheered. He'd shouted along with them, remembering how good it felt to yell.

Afterwards, though, he'd walked up to the tree and touched the bark. There were lots of bullet markings and he didn't know which one he had made. He felt like he should say sorry to the tree, then felt stupid.

Lots of the men had wanted to talk to him at first. They asked him questions about his group, about where he grew up, about the shitty people in his life that he must want to get back at. But even though Matthew had things to say, he found talking to everyone difficult. He always had. He'd mumble a few things about his mother and his sisters, and some of the men listened for a bit, but then lost interest.

He didn't tell anyone about Nabila. Part of him knew he should have, that she was a big part of why he was here. But he just couldn't. And he didn't want to hear these men say her name.

The morning air was already chilly. Matthew's left calf muscle was asleep, and he tried to move it, to shift it into a different position inside the sleeping bag. There wasn't much room, though. He wondered who had slept in the bag before him, how they had managed in the confined fabric. Then he wondered where they were now.

He lay there and thought about the winter, about what they'd do when it got really cold. Maybe they had plans to insulate the barn. So far the group had only been there when it was warm, so they hadn't had to worry about it. But someone must have a plan.

It was difficult to picture his old life. He tried to imagine his mother sitting in the kitchen, drinking coffee, walking past the entrance to his old room to check if he needed dinner. His sister tottering around in her heels, makeup and straightening irons all over the bathroom counter. His old job where he used to flip burgers, mix milkshakes, think about Nabila's face and the way her mouth looked when she said his name. He missed taking the bus home from work and listening to AJ talk. All of it seemed so far away now. It was another separate, distant reality.

Eventually people around Matthew started waking up and moving around. He waited for a while, until enough of them were out of their sleeping bags that he could blend in. He pulled on the same clothes he'd worn the night before and then went out to the back of the barracks where he peed and brushed his teeth. A couple of people nodded at him when he walked by, and it made him feel a bit better. He was still lonely, though.

He'd had to give up his phone when he arrived, and it felt strange not to have it with him. The general said they'd get them back sometimes if they wanted, because they were all brothers and they trusted each other. It's just that phones were distracting so they shouldn't have them all the time.

There was a rule that they couldn't tell anyone in the outside world where they were. It was an easy promise for Matthew to make because he wasn't exactly sure where he was himself.

Each day had to start with a run. It was raining a bit when the laps around the cornfield started, and Matthew tried to keep up as best as he could, but he wasn't used to running. His calf was cramping again, and he was still thirsty. But he knew AJ believed in him, so he kept going.

Once the running was over, there was the strength training. Someone had brought hand weights to the dead-grass area in front of the barracks, and everyone started lifting them and counting their reps. Some of the men were competing with each other. Matthew stayed at the edge of the group and lifted on his own. He'd grabbed the smallest weights that were there, but they were still too heavy.

The day went by slowly. Even though they were always moving, always going back and forth to the mess hall or to training, Matthew realized there wasn't all that much to do. He tried to talk to a few people, and some of them were friendly, but Matthew found that he didn't really have much to say.

He wondered if every day would be like this. He wondered what he had expected.

Eventually it was time for the group meeting. Matthew had been looking forward to it, because he'd always liked the meetings with AJ, and most of the time all Matthew had to do was listen. They all sat at the tables in the mess hall, and there was a small platform at the front. The general got up on the platform and the rest of the men got quiet.

Matthew shifted in his seat a bit because the man in front of him was blocking his view. He'd been too overwhelmed the night before to really pay attention to what the general looked like, and he was too far away now for Matthew to see his features. But he looked strong and he had a booming voice. Matthew sat up straight.

The general called out one man for good marksmanship, and everyone started pounding on the tables. It made Matthew jump at first, but then he joined in. It felt good. It was hard carrying around all the uncertainty and loneliness inside of him. It was easier to pound it out.

And then the general pointed to Matthew. Our newest recruit, he shouted, and then everyone was pounding on the tables again and the men on either side of him were pounding his back to congratulate him. Matthew was stunned at first. He didn't know what to do. But everyone was cheering, and he could feel the energy rising in his chest. He realized he was proud. He wasn't used to feeling like that.

There was a lot of noise, and Matthew was smiling. But then he saw Tom at the next table. His face didn't look kind. When Matthew looked at him again, he realized Tom was smirking. He was watching Matthew and tapping his fingers on the table.

Nabila didn't want to see Tierney the next morning. She stayed in her room until Tierney had gone downstairs, then waited in the war tree room until she heard that Tierney was busy with customers. When she was pulling the levers on the espresso machine and making drinks, Nabila walked through the hall to the front room and out the door. The floor squeaked, and the entrance bell rang. She was sure Tierney would have looked up and had seen her walking away, but she didn't glance back.

There was another café farther down the street, and Nabila sat there and ordered boiled eggs and toast and tea. The egg yolk was still a bit runny, and the tea had too much milk in it. There was an old lipstick stain on her fork. Matthew still hadn't texted.

She opened her phone and looked over their conversation. The last several messages were all from her, either asking him for an update or telling him that she was ready to meet him as soon as he was in town. Why didn't he just respond?

She'd messaged her undergraduate again, and she'd assured Nabila that everything was fine, that the kelp was being maintained within the strict conditions that Nabila had set out. She was wondering about external factors though, she'd told Nabila, about how next time they should maybe think about using a natural environment to see how other organisms and waves affected things.

Of course, Nabila had written back, saying that it was an obvious second phase. They needed to establish control rates first, though, for the next step to mean anything. These things took time.

Afterwards, she'd realized she'd been too sharp with the undergrad. Nabila ate her breakfast and thought about how her student was just eager, how she was actually quite constructive and had been thinking about the project's development. It was helpful to have a research assistant like that, even necessary. But it didn't make Nabila feel any better.

She'd taken her frustration out on her undergraduate when she was really angry with Tierney and Matthew. But when she thought a bit more about it, Nabila knew that she was also angry with herself. She'd allowed herself to be led along to the Fairytale Forest the night before without really thinking about things. She'd made assumptions about what was reasonable, about what she could have expected, but Tierney was operating with different standards. She should have noticed that.

Once they'd reached the edge of the forest and had made it back to the road, Tierney had started laughing. She was energized; her face flushed, her eyes dancing around in the dark. Nabila, though, hadn't been able to speak at first. She was out of breath, and a bit stunned, still trying to comprehend what had just happened and how close they'd been to disaster. The adrenaline that had gotten her through was fading and her arms were starting to sting with a hundred tiny cuts. Her calves were sore. She'd looked up at Tierney and Tierney had stopped laughing, had gotten serious.

"Look, it's fine, people sneak in all the time. They won't follow us past the fence. Even the dogs. I know."

"You knew they were going to chase us, didn't you?"

Tierney shrugged. "Sometimes they do. It's more to keep up appearances. You know, discourage people from sneaking in. I've never actually been caught."

"You should have told me."

"Look, I'm sorry. I didn't realize you'd get so freaked out."

Nabila took in a deep breath, had tried to steady her nerves. Things had worked out. Things were fine. But still.

They hadn't talked much on the train ride back, though Tierney had wanted to. She kept fidgeting, would bring up something they'd seen every now and then to see if it got any traction: first the swans, then the Ferris wheel, then the fairy statues, which they'd apparently passed on their way out but that Nabila hadn't even noticed.

Tierney had said that she felt badly, and there was a kind of desperation in her voice, like she couldn't stand it to have Nabila angry with her. She kept apologizing.

"It's okay," Nabila had eventually told her, but they both understood that it wasn't true quite yet.

Nabila was still upset this morning, but she also had a headache from the wine and wanted to hear from Matthew. And the previous evening had unsettled her. She'd always been good at observing things: in her research, she knew immediately when there was a change in vegetation patterns, or when a habitat was deteriorating. She'd thought she was good at noticing things. But now she was starting to wonder if maybe she wasn't quite as good at observing people.

She finished her breakfast and walked through parts of the city that used to be East Berlin, that still had old Soviet apartment blocks, massive and utilitarian, with small windows that looked out onto the streets below. Matthew was fine, she told herself. He couldn't write because he was in transit and maybe didn't have reception. It was what she'd expected, and the timeline was still fitting into what they'd talked about. She needed to remember that.

She'd become accustomed to worrying about him, though. It had crept up on her, so slowly that she hadn't really noticed it at first. After Matthew had left her lab that day she'd kept thinking about him, had kept replaying their interaction over and over in her head. Her harshness was necessary, she was sure, but he'd seemed so tender, and she felt like she'd snapped something inside of him. He'd walked away looking broken. Later that week, when he hadn't written, she'd told herself it was a good thing he'd gotten the message. But she hadn't felt very good about it herself.

He'd been quiet for another two weeks, and it was during that time that her concern had first really started. She'd found herself wishing he would write, just so she'd know he was okay, so she'd know that their last conversation hadn't done too much damage. Maybe he'd gone through with leaving, she wondered, the way he'd said he might. That could explain the silence.

And then something else had started to seep into her worry about him. It was the guilt again, and she kept trying to push it away because she didn't think she should feel like that, but instead of fading, it slowly grew. He was the one who had had expectations, she knew, and it wasn't her fault that she didn't feel the same way about him. But maybe she hadn't handled things very well. She'd always been able to shut Matthew down easily, even when she hadn't meant to. Maybe that time she'd been cruel.

Nabila had never thought of herself as a mean person, and that idea had unnerved her. She didn't like the way it made her feel. She became conscious of every interaction, of the way other people responded to her. She was extra courteous to cashiers, even began giving up change when asked on street corners. Nabila could tell she was overthinking things. But that knowledge didn't really change anything, didn't make her feel any better.

She should have been kinder, she'd eventually decided. There could have been a way to let Matthew know that she didn't want anything more than a friendship but that she still cared about him, that she cared about what he did and how he felt. That she still wanted to help him. That's how she should have approached their conversation, she realized. She could have figured out a way to do it.

When three weeks had passed and he still hadn't written, she'd thought about apologizing. She remembered how his face had looked as he'd left her laboratory, small and dejected, and it was the same expression he'd have in their forest when she'd shut his suggestions down. Soon he'd hardly ever make suggestions to their game, and she'd learned that she had the power to dictate what they did. That with her words she was able to lift him up or smother him. She used to get upset in high school when she saw others manipulate him, when she noticed them play upon his susceptibilities. But she realized she'd done the same.

So she'd written to him. It had been a short text, nothing too dramatic, just saying that she was sorry for the way their last conversation had gone, and that she hoped he was doing okay. She asked if he'd ended up moving. If so, she said she hoped he liked the place.

She'd sent it on a Wednesday, and by the Sunday he still hadn't written back. Nabila had become alarmed. For some reason the idea that Matthew could have committed suicide got stuck in her mind, and she couldn't get it out. There was no real reason to think that was what had happened, no indication, but his fragility had somehow made it seem plausible. She found his sister, Roxanne, online, wanted to see if she'd posted anything. But there was nothing about Matthew anywhere. Roxanne just had pictures from the club she worked at, ads for ladies' night and bar specials.

And then finally, after two and a half weeks, he responded. She'd been in the library reading a research paper when his message had come through, and she'd sat there for a moment, stared at it. She'd resigned herself to the fact that he wasn't going to answer, that whatever strange friendship they'd had was now over. But then there was Matthew, suddenly writing her back.

She opened up the text and his note was curt. He had done it and gone, he'd said, and he was now far away. Nabila had made it clear that she didn't care what he did, he said, so he wasn't sure why she was asking.

Nabila had left the library and had gone to the lakeshore, walked the pier. The wind had been cold and the water was crashing against the breakwater. She figured he probably had a right to be upset, that she hadn't treated him very well. All she'd wanted for so long was a note, and she thought that getting one back would make things easier. But now that she knew he was upset and probably still stinging from what she'd said, it added a new layer of guilt.

She responded to Matthew and asked him where he'd moved to and what he was doing there. She hoped it was good for him, she'd said. She was sorry again about their last conversation, she wrote, and of course she cared about what happened to him, because he was her friend. She hadn't meant to come across so severely.

Then she waited, again. Days went by. He didn't respond.

Nabila decides that Matthew should come up with an idea for the game. She realizes she never wonders about what he's thinking or what he wants, and that maybe, with a little bit of prodding, he'll be able to add something interesting to the story. She usually likes to set things her own way, but she suddenly begins to wonder what it would be like if she didn't know everything about their forest.

She starts small. She asks him what kind of animals he thinks there would be in the city after the sea levels rose. At first he just stares at her. Then he asks her what she thinks. Nabila sighs.

"Just think, Matthew," she tells him. "What kind of animals do you want there to be? Elephants?" she asks when he doesn't respond.

"I guess."

"You guess?"

"Well," he says. He pulls leaves off a shrub and piles them at his feet. "Well, it might be weird with elephants. They can't climb to the top of the buildings. And then they'd drown."

Nabila nods. "Okay then," she says. "Makes sense. What animals would be left?"

Matthew picks up a leaf and inspects it, then brings it to his nose. He smells it carefully. "I don't think there would be a lot of animals," he says. He looks at her quickly, then looks away again. "I think most of the animals would run to the tops of hills, not to the tops of buildings. So we wouldn't see a lot of animals."

Of course, Nabila thinks. That seems right. She should ask him a different question.

She watches him start to tap the leaf against his nose, and begin staring off somewhere above her head. Then he turns back to her. "The only animals that I think we'd see," he says, then pauses for a moment, takes a little breath. "I think they'd be water animals. Because when the sea rises, they'll come in with the ocean."

"What do you mean?"

"Well," he says, and rests his hand in his lap with the leaf inside it. "Well, if the water takes over the city so that the bottoms of the buildings are all covered, then we'll have all the big ocean animals swimming down the street. There will be great white sharks. And whales. We can look over the edge of the building and see them swimming around."

Nabila looks at Matthew, impressed. "Of course."

He smiles slowly, watches her carefully.

"Our building is like an island in the middle of the ocean," she says. "When we look down over the edge, there's got to be ocean animals." She gets up and runs toward the wall at the back of the garden. It's concrete, but she pretends it's made of glass. "Look Matthew!" she says. She points down at the street.

Matthew watches her for a moment, then drops his leaf and joins her at the wall. "See the dolphin?" Nabila says. "It's jumping!"

Matthew stares at the wall, his eyes searching. He glances at Nabila. "What do you see?" she asks.

He looks back at the concrete. "A turtle?" he says.

"A giant turtle!"

"Yeah." He nods his head. "It's swimming around."

"And look!" Nabila says, pointing to the wall again. "There's a humpback! You can see how long it is under the water!"

"And maybe it sprays water up into the air like a fountain?" Matthew asks.

"Of course!"

Matthew smiles. He turns back to the wall and places both his hands flat against it. Then he rests his forehead on the concrete too. "Look, Nabila!" he suddenly whispers. "See what's there at the end of that street? Coming toward us. It's a pirate ship."

Nabila doesn't expect this from him. There is an ugly feeling inside her, like she'd been cruel without realizing it. She puts her hands against the concrete too. "What does it look like?" she asks.

"It's tall and made of wood and there's a mermaid on the front," he says. "A carved mermaid, you know, leading the ship. And it has the flag with the skull and crossbones."

"The Jolly Roger," Nabila corrects.

"Yeah, the Jolly Roger. That's right."

"Well," she says, "they better watch out for sirens. They're probably here too."

"Sirens?" Matthew asks. "Are there still police cars?"

"No, silly." Nabila laughs. "They're beautiful mermaids who sing so that pirates sail toward them, and then their ship crashes on the rocks."

Matthew stares at Nabila with his mouth slightly open. "That's so mean."

She shrugs. "They're pirates."

"Still."

Matthew looks back toward the concrete, then over at Nabila again. She watches his eyelashes flutter. He picks another leaf off the ground and starts ripping it to pieces and dropping them on his thigh. "Why are girls so mean?" he says.

"What?" Nabila sits up straight and crosses her arms. "We're not mean."

"Sometimes," Matthew says. He gathers the leaf pieces together and collects them in his palm. He doesn't look up at Nabila.

"Men are meaner," she says. "Do you know that they didn't let women vote for the longest time?"

Matthew stays quiet. He transfers the broken leaf from one hand to the other and then back again. Nabila suddenly notices that he has freckles on the backs of his hands.

"I know your sisters can be mean," she says. "It's just because there's two of them. They gang up on you."

"They don't like me."

"Of course they like you."

"They say I look like my dad." Matthew wipes his nose with the back of his wrist, and Nabila sees a shiny bit of mucus when he brings it away.

"It's true. I do look like my dad. There's a picture of him when he was a kid, and for a long time I thought it was a picture of me. He's sitting in the park and holding this little navy boat. I kept asking my mom where that toy was. I didn't realize it was my dad."

"That's funny."

"They don't like him." Matthew stares down into the dirt. The skin across his temple is almost translucent, and Nabila can see the outline of a tiny blue vein. "There were still some old shirts of his in one of the closets, and last summer my sisters took them out to the parking lot behind the apartment building, stuffed them in a bucket and burned them. It smelled so bad because the bucket got burnt, too. They say that he's probably dead by now and that would be the best news they'd ever get."

Nabila uncrosses her arms and lets them rest on her lap. "What does your mom say?" she asks.

"She doesn't talk about him. But one time she told me that we had to forget him."

Nabila crosses and uncrosses her fingers and stares at her knees. She takes a quick look up at Matthew, and he takes the bits of leaf and scatters them one by one in a circle around him. The wind is blowing, and it keeps trying to pull the pieces out of his hand.

"I just... I just always think," Matthew says slowly, "about how we don't really know where he is. And how he could be doing something different or amazing and maybe we should stop being mad at him. But whenever I say that, they start yelling. They don't like that idea."

"So you think that he could have become a soldier?"

Matthew looks up quickly. "He is a soldier." His eyes fill with tears as he looks at her, and Nabila has to glance away. She picks at some dirt caught under her nail.

After what seems like a long time, she says, "Let's look at the water again." She goes back over to the wall and leans against the concrete. "Come on. Let's see where the pirates went."

She hears Matthew sniffling, but a moment later he sits next to her. She raises her hands to her eyes and pretends to look through a telescope. He does the same.

At the meetings back home, AJ had talked about guns, but it was about control, he'd said, in simply having that power. It had sounded incredible to Matthew. People respected you when you were stronger than them, AJ told him. Matthew believed it. He wondered what having that kind of power felt like.

The men around him seemed to come by that power naturally. They talked about the rush of shooting something, of how good it felt to finally be in charge. They competed over who could do more push-ups.

Matthew felt quiet around them. He already knew he was a bit softer than the other men there, not quite as hard-edged, not quite as accustomed to violence. He'd never been able to handle aggression very well; when someone started shouting, he always felt like he was five years old again, hiding in his bedroom closet. And everyone here seemed to shout a lot. In his training he tried to move and yell the way he was told to, the way they wanted him to, but he found it difficult, especially when he was so tired. Sometimes he'd fall to the ground and would press hard on his knees but would still have trouble getting up.

He thought about Nabila a lot. In the meetings some of the men talked about their reasons for being there, and she was a big part of his, he realized, part of the reason why he'd ended up where he was. She'd made him angrier than he'd ever been before—angrier than he used to be with his sisters when they'd lock him in the bathroom by holding the handle on the other side of the door, angrier than he'd be at his mother when she used to forget to pack his school lunch and he'd have to pretend he wasn't hungry. When his training became unbearable, when he couldn't run any faster, or focus any longer, he thought of Nabila in her laboratory, pretending that her stocks of seaweed were more important than everything he ever was. That memory always helped him along.

Then she'd sent him a message. Matthew couldn't believe it at first, and he figured that it must have been a joke. That she was continuing to toy with him. He knew he was smarter now, and wasn't ready to fall for her tricks. He ignored it and had written to AJ instead, thanking him for his help, asking if he or any other members of their meetings would be joining him soon. The men here were decent, he said, but it would be nice to see some familiar faces.

He hadn't heard back.

There hadn't been anything from AJ since he first arrived actually, when he sent Matthew a note of congratulations. Everyone at headquarters got to check their phones three times a week, any more than that and the phones were too distracting, the general had said. The phones were locked up and kept by the general the rest of the time. Every time Matthew got his phone back, he checked for a note from AJ, but there was nothing. Matthew wondered if he was mad at him. He couldn't figure out why he would be, though.

In the meantime, Matthew continued training. Every day was filled with running and shooting and listening to people talk, being ready to try to respond if someone asked him a question. It exhausted him.

It was better to be here, everyone said, better to be fighting for something real rather than toiling away in a society that didn't appreciate them, and that made sense to Matthew. There hadn't been much to flipping burgers and making milkshakes. It hadn't been important. But he did think about how the job had been easy. Part of him worried that he wouldn't be able to keep up here.

He thought he might also be homesick, which made him angry, because he wasn't supposed to be feeling like that. He hadn't liked his old home. He'd always wished he were somewhere else. But AJ hadn't answered his messages, and he didn't have email addresses for any of the other men at the meetings. He knew his mom and sisters were relieved to have him out of the way. He had no other friends. Except Nabila maybe, but he was supposed to hate her. It was confusing.

He could also tell that some of the men there didn't like him. They usually punched each other's arms to say hi, but whenever Matthew was there, they punched him a lot harder. Then they'd laugh when he'd wince. Tom's punches were the worst. He'd also laugh when Matthew couldn't shoot straight at the trees during practice. Matthew couldn't do anything right.

One time Tom had played a joke on him. It had been the middle of the night, and two of the other men had woken him up and told him that the general needed him right away. But instead of taking him to the general's quarters, they took him to the firing range.

The moon was bright enough that Matthew could see Tom standing there with a rifle as they walked up. He was smiling like he had on their first car ride, a kind of crazy, toothy grin, and he told Matthew that he was going to help him become a better shot. Tom was going to demonstrate how it was done, and Matthew was going to have a front-row seat so he could really learn.

Matthew didn't say anything. The other two men marched him over to the trees and pushed his back up against one. Then someone pulled out a rope and tied him to the trunk. He started to shake.

Matthew's hands were pressed against the bark, and he could feel the cuts of bullet holes, the rough spaces where the tree had tried to repair itself. Tom fumbled with the gun, and Matthew could see the metal shining in the moonlight.

"Don't worry, I'm an excellent shot," Tom said, and then laughed with all his teeth out.

Matthew could hear the blood rushing through his ears. He swallowed. Nobody would care if Tom shot him, he realized. The group had other men. AJ had other recruits. His mother would just think he decided never to come home. He tried to move his hands but the rope was pulled taut.

"I'm gonna teach you a thing or two about aim," Tom called out.

Matthew bit his bottom lip and stayed very still. Nabila would know something happened. She would make sure people looked for him, would maybe even come to the farm to find his body for herself. He pictured her with a shovel in hand, digging up dry dirt, her hair pulled back in a ponytail.

"See? This is how you do it," Tom called. "Look at my legs. Look at my shoulders. I've got the shot aimed right for your forehead."

Matthew heard himself swallow again and again. He wanted to close his eyes but couldn't even move his lids. His hands gripped the bark. One of his fingers caught on a bullet hole.

"And boom! That would be it," Tom said. He jerked the rifle up and Matthew screamed, then Tom laughed. The rifle was at his side now. He hadn't fired anything. Matthew tried to close his mouth but he was breathing too heavily.

"Fuck, man. You think I would really shoot you?" He laughed again. Then he got serious. He walked up to Matthew, put his face right up to Matthew's nose.

"I don't know what AJ thought he saw in you," he hissed.

Then he pushed the barrel of the rifle up against Matthew's stomach, and Matthew couldn't breathe again.

"You need to man the fuck up," he said. "It was just a joke. Don't you know how to take a fucking joke?"

His voice was inside Matthew's head, taunting him. But it wasn't Tom anymore. It had turned into his father's voice, a memory from long ago when Matthew was sitting on the kitchen linoleum. His father was standing over him.

"You need to man the fuck up."

Roxanne had taken something from him. Or he was waiting for her to do something, he couldn't remember. He was sad and upset and cold and that's why he was crying. His father had come in and found him sobbing on the floor.

"Man. The fuck. Up."

The gun was pressing into his stomach and Tom was laughing in his ear. Matthew wanted to die. This place was supposed to be better but it wasn't because there was Tom, because there was always someone like Tom. Nothing he did would make any difference. And Nabila was never there.

Then the gun was gone.

His hands were untied now and they landed on the grass. And then Matthew vomited on them.

"Fuck man. What's wrong with you?"

Matthew didn't know.

He could hear the other two men walking away, could hear the dried grass under their feet. Tom still stood over him. "You make us all look bad," he said. "You're a fucking liability."

He didn't know what Tom wanted. He knew that he wanted Nabila, but also that he didn't want her, and also that she would never have him. Tom was still standing there and Matthew's hands were covered in vomit.

And then Tom was walking away. Suddenly Matthew was alone, the sound of footsteps fading. He moved his fingers. He rubbed the vomit onto the grass and cleaned his nails, tried to ignore the burning of his throat and his pounding abdomen.

It took a long time for him to stand up. When he finally did, he turned around and put his hands on the tree bark. He thought about the garden on top of the building with Nabila, about what being there used to feel like. There was always the sound of the leaves in the wind and the smell of car exhaust. He remembered being mostly happy there with her, or at least not worried, not afraid. For a moment he felt safe again.

Matthew heard the call of night birds, and he pulled his hands away from the tree, started to walk back toward the barracks barn. He wasn't in a rush to get there though. His nose was plugged, so he breathed through his mouth. He wished he had a tissue.

The next day he decided to respond to Nabila. He wasn't sure that he should, but he didn't really know what he was doing anymore, didn't know if anything even mattered. Tom had probably told everyone about him throwing up and they would all be laughing at him. He wanted to write to Nabila and show her that he was angry, because she was the reason that he'd ended up in this place. She was the reason the other men were making fun of him.

But he also missed her terribly. He wanted to talk to her, to just say something, really anything. All he wanted to do was make contact.

So when he got his phone time the next day, he responded to her message. He just said that he was fine, and that he didn't know why Nabila cared anyway. He didn't want to seem eager. He was still unsure if she was trying to make fun of him like AJ had said, and he didn't know what he'd do if her response was to laugh at him. He thought about maybe going into the trees and shooting himself.

Then he turned his phone off before putting it back in the box with the rest of them. He didn't think they would check them, he hadn't given them his passcode, but he didn't want them to find Nabila's messages. No one had given him clear rules, but he knew he wasn't supposed to be talking to her.

Matthew thought about her a lot the next two days. He wondered if she was thinking about him too, and he figured that he wanted her to. He was angry and then hopeful and then angry again because he didn't want to be hopeful.

But Nabila didn't laugh at him. In two days, when he got his phone again, he saw that she'd responded immediately to his note. She wanted to make sure he was okay, she said, and she was worried he wasn't; he'd left without really explaining where he was going.

For a few moments he was so happy. But then he didn't know what do to. AJ had warned him about how Nabila would try to manipulate him, how she'd tell him things that he wanted to hear and then take them back. She'd already done that, he knew. He reminded himself how furious he was with her, how unfairly she'd treated him.

He thought maybe she was trying to play with him. So he didn't respond right away. He thought about it, turned the possibilities over and over in his mind. AJ would have known what to do, but he'd stopped talking to Matthew. And everyone at headquarters had started to ignore him.

If he wrote back to Nabila and she didn't respond, there would be nothing left. So he decided to wait.

He tried to focus on the training instead. He was at the firing range one day, getting ready to aim at the crooked tree off to the left, when it happened. Suddenly there was pain exploding at his knee, shooting all the way up and down his right leg. He couldn't think straight. It burned so hot that for a moment he thought it might be cold, like when he was a kid and he'd stepped on the frozen pond and his foot had gone right through. He'd screamed, but it was only just above his ankle and his sisters had told him to step out.

He saw stars, alternations of black and white. Maybe he was sideways on the ground. Things were completely silent, but he could see people moving.

Then all the sound came rushing back into his head and he felt like he was falling. His ears throbbed. The fire in his leg burned on, and he tried to look, to see where it was, but he couldn't figure out what the shapes around him were. So instead he put his hand on his belly, then down to his hip, then across the front of his thigh. He felt cloth and skin, and when he brought his fingers back up to his face they were red.

His head was full of memories. The night before he'd put his foot through the pond ice, Libby had painted his toenails red. He'd been sleeping, and when he woke up he found that they'd hidden the nail polish remover. He'd gone to school and forgotten about it, but later that day when his foot was in the water, when the pain of the cold was shooting all the way up his body, he'd imagined his toes in his boots bloody.

He turned his head, lifted his neck, and looked down across his body. There was a red hole in his leg. It was just above his knee.

He tried to sit up, but there was pain in his stomach; it was like he couldn't breathe. He felt the air get stuck in his nose. And it was only then that he felt scared, felt himself gasping. He tasted smoke in the space all around him.

Soldiers got killed in battle all the time, he told himself. And he thought that dying would have been better than his loneliness in this place. But now he was terrified.

He moved his hand downward, touched his thigh again. Then he heard himself scream, felt the sound vibrate through his chest.

It bothered him that he couldn't focus, that he kept thinking of being a kid again, walking home with the water sloshing inside his boots and starting to turn to ice. In the apartment they'd had to thaw his feet by the open oven before they could remove his socks. Warming his toes back up had hurt so much that all he could do was sit there on the floor and cry. He touched the linoleum where it curled up beneath the cupboard. Roxanne had said she'd get him a fresh pair of socks, but she must have forgotten.

Then his father was there, his head blocking the kitchen light. Man. The fuck. Up. Matthew couldn't move.

There was someone standing over him now. They were blocking out the sun, and they moved their hand and he couldn't tell if they were reaching for their weapon. He tried to remember where he'd been standing before he fell, who'd been around him. He couldn't quite figure it out.

Someone was behind him now too, and then he felt their hands on his shoulders. He tried to ask for help. A sound came out of his mouth but he didn't recognize it, couldn't connect it to anything that should have come from his own body. He could only feel the pain, the way it shot up and down, burst into tiny fragments like bonfire sparks. They were scattered all over his legs, but now also his belly, his forehead. They were the orange of the oven element. The sparks pulsed and pushed and grew, flowed down across his knee, and he knew he wouldn't be able to stand up.

It was difficult to think straight, but he tried anyway, tried to remember the names of the men who were now holding him up, carrying him across the grass. He tried to think of his mother's phone number, why they'd had to hide from airplanes in Nabila's forest. Nothing was coming easy. There was smoke in his head and heat in his bones, red and orange and burnt bronze.

When two weeks had gone by and Matthew hadn't responded to her second message, Nabila found herself completely consumed by a need to hear back. She felt involved now with whatever was going on with him. She couldn't just walk away and leave things. So she wrote to him again.

She'd felt horrible, felt like she'd read things all wrong and now had to fix it. She wanted him to stop being angry with her. In her note she told Matthew that they didn't have to keep talking if he didn't want to, but that he needed to know she was sorry. That she didn't want him to continue being upset. Were things better now, was he doing okay? If she knew that he was fine, she thought, that might be enough.

It took a few days, but this time he got back to her. He still wasn't sure that she really cared, he'd said, but the place wasn't as great as he'd thought it would be. That he was exhausted all the time because he never got enough sleep. And now his leg was hurt.

He wouldn't tell her where he was exactly, just that he'd joined a kind of new society, and there were leaders who told the rest of them what to do. Because he was new, he was still in training, which was difficult. He was learning to fight like a soldier, he'd said, but it was harder than he'd thought. He'd been injured in an exercise, and was still recovering from that. He was staying in an old building and it was cold at night. There were only showers every other day, and even then, not a lot of hot water. He missed home.

The message had terrified Nabila. Up until that point Matthew had been vague about everything, but now she realized that his trip wasn't a simple relocation: he'd gone somewhere where he was living apart from everyone else, and she didn't understand what kind of group he was talking about. It wouldn't be easy to leave, though. That kind of group never was. And he was unhappy.

It was then that Nabila really regretted that day at the lab. She'd decided back in high school that she had a responsibility for him, that she had an obligation to try to help. But instead she'd done the opposite. If she'd said something different in the lab, maybe just a sentence or two, Matthew would have stayed. She could have asked him questions. It would have all been so simple.

She wrote back and asked what kind of place he was living in, and he responded after only a few days this time, said they were on some land far away from other people, near some old farms. He said it was like living on the edge of the world. He'd flown into Berlin but he didn't know exactly where they were now, because they'd driven for a while afterwards. The new recruits, like him, weren't allowed to leave the headquarters at all. Now, Matthew said, after being there for weeks, it was as if everything beyond their land no longer existed.

His message went on for quite a while that time, and he told Nabila about how there were people from all over the world there. They thought the same way he did, he said. They didn't try to ignore the obvious problems with the rest of society. For the first time in his life, he said, he was living with people who were able to understand him.

Everything she heard worried Nabila. And she wondered if he was trying to make his situation appear better than it actually was. Maybe he wanted it to seem like he was able to handle things when he actually didn't know what to do.

Do you like where you are? she'd written back. Do you want to stay?

He'd responded a few days later. He wasn't sure.

They messaged regularly now, every few days, and though Matthew no longer seemed angry with her, Nabila felt responsible when he talked about how strange and difficult his life had become. Their group only had the basics, he said, because it was new, and they had to work hard. They were working to make the world the way it should be, Matthew told her, and she didn't ask for specifics, only wondered what he'd been convinced of.

She realized she was too involved now. Part of her wished she hadn't been so persistent, because it had started to feel like a kind of mission, like rescuing Matthew was her new focus. She waited for his texts, wanted to understand more about what he was doing. He had never been good with details and she scoured his messages for anything of significance.

Nabila couldn't concentrate on her work. She was no longer able to immerse herself in her research, in her world of plants and water that she usually fell into. And she found herself increasingly worried about him.

She asked if anyone else knew that he was there. Had he told his mother and his sisters? Any of his other friends?

No, he replied. His mother and sisters thought he was travelling through Europe. Besides Nabila, all of his friends were also in the group.

This time, when Nabila asked if he was happy there, he'd said he didn't think so. That he was scared. And then he'd asked her if there was any way she could help him get home.

For a moment she wondered if he still wanted her, if this was some-how a ploy to get her to go to him. Maybe he was creating an elaborate story and lying about all of these things. It could be a trick.

But then she remembered that this was Matthew. She didn't think he could be making it all up.

Part of Nabila was also aware that she wanted to believe him, because this was her chance to make things better. She hadn't saved Matthew the first time he'd asked for help, and though she had no idea how to help him now, she had to try.

She asked him if it was safe to continue communicating over text, and he said yes, that he hadn't given them his phone passcode.

Nabila wasn't exactly sure that meant their messages were safe, but she realized that the group hadn't stopped him from texting her so far. Maybe they didn't care much about that. And she figured she had no option but to keep talking to Matthew.

As long as he hadn't hurt anyone, she'd help him, she said. He promised that he'd just been in training, and she couldn't imagine him lying. She also couldn't imagine him violent.

Matthew told her that he just wanted to go home.

So she began helping him figure out a plan. Nabila asked about where he was staying, about how many people were there, and he told her about barracks where everyone slept in the middle of old farm fields. There were roads in the distance, he told her, far away but close enough that he could see them when he stood on a nearby hill. He remembered the drive from Berlin had been a few hours.

Nabila decided that he should leave at night. When everyone else was asleep, she said, he should pretend to go to the washroom. Then he could hike out to the road, walk along it until he could hitch a ride somewhere. When everyone woke up in the morning he'd be gone.

It could take him a few days to get to Berlin, she explained to him, because he had to find a driver who was headed there. But sooner or later there should be someone.

Matthew liked the plan. He was worried that someone would come after him, because he couldn't walk very fast with his injured leg, but Nabila figured he'd be okay as long as he walked the fields at night, and didn't talk to too many people on his way to the city. She knew that Matthew always did a good job of blending into the background anyway.

But then he wrote back that he didn't know how he'd get to Canada, because the group had taken away his passport. Everyone had to hand over their documents when they arrived; it was one of the rules. He had no idea where it was.

Nabila was upset when she heard that. They'd had such a clear plan, and this was going to make it more complicated.

He really needed her help, she realized. Matthew had always been oblivious to what was going on around him, and maybe he hadn't realized the consequences of what he'd done. No one else was looking out for him.

He'd have to apply for a new one, she told him, once he was in Berlin. He could go to the embassy and explain that it had been stolen. It might take a few days. Did he have some money, she asked, for a hotel or a hostel? He'd need a place to stay.

But he had a second passport, he said. A British one, because his dad was from London. His mother had made him renew it when she heard he was going to Europe, but he didn't think he'd need it, so he'd left it at home. Would that work? he asked her.

Nabila was relieved. Yes, she told him. That was perfect. Then he wouldn't need to wait for new documents in Berlin.

He said the passport was in his room in his mother's apartment. Could she get it for him?

Nabila asked him to try to remember exactly where it was. She could mail it to the British embassy so he could pick it up when he got there, she thought. She started typing that out, but then stopped herself.

What if the embassy staff started questioning him? What if he started talking about his Canadian passport, and how this group he'd joined had taken it away? The thought of him sitting in a room, detained indefinitely, gave her pause. He wouldn't know what to do, wouldn't know what to say or not say, and she didn't want him to get in more trouble than he already was. All he wanted to do now was come home.

She thought of all the times kids used to make fun of Matthew. Even Nabila, who'd never really meant to hurt him, knew she had. Very few people ever stood up for him. And even now, she realized, there wasn't anyone else willing to save him.

So she said she'd bring it to him herself.

This would make up for everything else, Nabila thought. It was just a little bit of help, something that might give Matthew a second chance. It didn't feel wrong. For a moment she wondered if helping him come back could be dangerous, but then she remembered how fragile he'd been when she last saw him. She didn't know what the group was all about, but she knew that he wasn't like the other people who were there, that he'd just gotten caught up in it and wasn't sure how to extract himself.

All she was going to do was bring him the passport. She wouldn't do anything else, nothing extreme, she thought, but nothing like that would be needed. So she felt okay with it.

And Matthew seemed relieved when she told him. He said he'd follow her plan, and that he wanted to leave soon. He wanted to get away.

Nabila said she'd figure it out. She was going to take care of things.

Nabila stayed out all afternoon, putting off going back to the café and seeing Tierney. She walked and walked and stopped for some food, then walked some more. She hated feeling like Matthew was wasting her time. But there was nothing else she could do, nothing to get ready for or prepare for. So she resigned herself to being a tourist.

She'd been walking along the river when she heard a commotion on the bridge ahead of her. A crowd was gathering along the railing, and they were looking at something on the other side, staring and pointing.

She saw bright-blue pipes as she approached, the colour of robins' eggs, set up along the riverbank. They looked so strange, so whimsical, that she wondered at first if they were part of the set-up for the nearby Christmas market, if they were part of some larger scene. But then she remembered how she'd read about the groundwater pipes, how they were either pink or blue and stood out from the buildings around them. They were redirecting water into the river.

Nabila joined the crowd on the bridge and stared out toward the pipes where construction workers were pulling something out of a hole in the ground. She heard the sound of a small machine coming from inside it. The noise was coming from a chainsaw, Nabila realized.

A few minutes later the sound stopped, and the workers started lifting something out of the hole.

It was a section of tree root. People on the bridge started talking as it emerged. It was solid, about half a foot across and nearly five feet long. It took three men to lift it out and it kept shedding dirt onto their shoulders.

The soil beneath city pavement was compacted, Nabila knew, and was difficult for tree roots to navigate. Around a water pipe, though, the soil was looser because it had been disturbed. Trees sought out such places, tried to let their roots take hold along the metal so that they could get a good grip in the ground. But that could block the pipe.

The workers laid the root on the riverbank next to another two sections that they'd already pulled out. Nabila saw the tree then. It was several metres back from the river, close to the nearby sidewalk and beside an apartment building. It was large for a city tree. But she noticed that they had a truck parked beside it, a spray-painted marking on the trunk in the form of a large X.

Once a tree had found a water pipe, it would always try to find its way back. It was like a bear that had gotten used to human food.

Removing a tree was no easy operation. And not a simple solution, Nabila knew, since even small parts of the roots could go on living after the trunk and the leaves were detached. She wondered if the tree could sense the danger.

And then she wondered about herself, if she could sense danger, trust her instincts. She wanted to think she could. But she'd never really been tested. And her lack of concern when they went to the Fairytale Forest made her question things.

When she'd met with Roxanne to get Matthew's passport, she'd been careful. She'd told a colleague where she was going, told her exactly what time she should be back to the lab. It wasn't Roxanne she was worried about so much as who else she wondered might be in the apartment or the building.

But things had been fine; there hadn't been anything to worry about. All the caution hadn't really been necessary. Roxanne had met her outside the building, just as they'd planned, rode the elevator up with her. Roxanne had been sleeping because she worked nights, was wearing sweatpants and a sweatshirt in different shades of grey. She barely acknowledged Nabila; she looked at her with mild irritation, but mostly just disinterest. When they got up to the apartment, she pointed out Matthew's room and then disappeared back into hers.

Nabila had messaged Roxanne online and reintroduced herself, told her she was going to Europe for vacation and Matthew wanted some things from home. Roxanne didn't ask any questions. She didn't even seem to remember Nabila that well. She'd given her a time and Nabila had made sure she was there.

Matthew had always come to Nabila's building, so it was the first time she'd ever been to his apartment. She remembered feeling upset at how small it was. Libby had moved out, but there still weren't enough bedrooms, so they had curtains blocking off part of the living room where Matthew had slept. There was only one bathroom, the table in the kitchen just had two chairs. It was piled with takeout containers and papers.

She could hear the TV being turned on from Roxanne's room, a laugh track spilling out into the hallway. Nabila pulled back the curtain and peered into Matthew's space.

She remembers being thrilled by that moment, by the secrecy of it. It was always strange to be in someone's room without them. He'd left socks on the floor, half a bottle of water near the single bed. The sheets were pulled up over the pillow in an attempt to make things neat, but it all still looked disarrayed.

There were no windows, but a shaft of light from the hallway lit things up enough to see. Matthew had a nightstand and a small dresser, and on the wall a poster of a movie featuring a group of men in tactical gear holding guns. She recognized his uniform from the fast food place crumpled in a pile in the corner, and another pair of pants was hanging off the edge of his bed. The space smelled faintly of weed, sweat and greasy food.

In the corner of the room there was a pile of things—mail, old flyers, papers—and that's where he said it would be. It took a while; she had to take things out of the pile, lay them on the floor. She found old application forms for different jobs, mostly restaurants, but also a gardening service and the army. And then there were old papers that looked like notes from high school classes, and that's where she found the passport, tucked in between science formulas. She checked that it was his picture. His hair was slicked back in the shot, and his eyes were wide, as if he'd been surprised by the camera. She closed it back up, stuck it in her purse.

Nabila stood up, and then paused for a moment, looked around the room again. She tried to imagine Matthew here, waking up, bits of light from the living room sliding past the edges of the curtain. She wondered about the kinds of things he liked doing. She realized she had no idea. She wasn't sure she'd ever known.

Nabila stepped out of the space and pulled the curtain back across his room. She wasn't sure if she'd tell the truth if Roxanne asked what she was getting, but she never asked, so Nabila hadn't needed to worry about it. She stood by the doorway for a minute, then called goodbye. Roxanne didn't respond. So she'd just left.

Just as it had felt strange to be in Matthew's room, it felt strange to carry around his document. Nabila wished she could just hand it over and then have her hands clean, not have to worry about things. She wanted to pass on the responsibility.

Nabila stood in the middle of the crowd for a long time and watched the crew deal with the tree roots. They took out more chainsaws, and the buzz from them seemed louder than it should have been. The air seemed to vibrate around Nabila.

A couple of kids next to her were watching with wide eyes, whispering to each other in German. The workers raised their chainsaws up, poised them over the pieces of wood, and then rushed down at the roots and began to slice through.

Wood chips flew everywhere, like sparks.

The roots fell apart quickly, sectioned off into neat pieces of firewood. The kids next to her talked louder so they could hear each other over the noise.

Nabila watched the tree, the crown that still held a few yellow leaves. She wondered if it felt pain.

Even though the crew had cut up these roots, and even if they did take away the whole tree, there must still be long tendrils of root snaking through the dirt, Nabila knew. They would be spread out in different directions that the workers wouldn't be able to get to.

The kids left, but Nabila stood there for a little while longer. She watched the workers pile up the sections of destroyed root, and the sky began to grow overcast, the air cool. Farther down the river, she could see a bit of rain falling onto the water. The wind was blowing in her direction, and she knew if she didn't move she was going to get wet.

After the accident, they put Matthew in a small building on the outskirts of the training grounds. They just called the building "medical," and one of the recruits who had been a doctor before he'd arrived had taken the bullet out of Matthew's leg and stitched up the hole. The doctor told him all that afterwards, because he hadn't remembered any of it: they'd given him pills and he'd been out cold for almost a day.

It took him a while to recover. They gave him painkillers and served him food at his bed, exempted him from training. For the first time since he'd arrived, Matthew felt almost cheerful. He could hear the training drills in the distance, and was alone most of the time, but that was okay because it meant no one was there to bother him.

His thigh was hidden under an inch of bandages, which the doctor changed every day. When the doctor unravelled them, Matthew could see the red part of his leg where flesh had been gouged out. It was starting to scab over.

The doctor said Matthew had gotten lucky, that the bullet hadn't hit his bone or lodged in his leg. But it had torn up part of his muscle. It would always be misshapen.

They gave him more pills, and the pills were wonderful, and Matthew thought that this was the way to go, if he were ever to do it, because they made him barely feel his body. It was like clouds, some kind of mist, and it settled over him and calmed him down. He felt so good that the next time he was given his phone privileges, he decided to respond to Nabila, to tell her things that had happened. If she didn't get back to him, he'd just get more painkillers.

But she did get back to him, almost immediately. So he responded again. He told her about all the good things about this place, about the bigger goals he was now part of and why it was so important. And then he also told her about the awful parts. He told her his leg was hurt, that he didn't have any friends here. That some days he was unsure about what he was doing.

He was dreamy while on the painkillers and angry if they started to wear off before he got more. He tried walking on his leg, but he couldn't get more than a few steps at a time, and he needed a cane. The doctor told him he wouldn't be able to run for a long time. After that, Matthew went back to bed and wouldn't get up.

Soldiers had to run, Matthew knew. He wasn't of any use now. He couldn't do anything, couldn't be of any use to the group. And they wouldn't let him stay in medical forever. He'd have to leave, but he didn't know how he could get home.

He told Nabila all of this. Every time he got his phone he'd have messages waiting from her, and sometimes when he'd write back she'd respond right away and they could have a conversation in real time. Talking to her always made him feel better. And she made him think about where he was and what he was doing. He realized he wouldn't be able to be part of the group the way he wanted to. Soon he realized he wanted to go home.

When he shared that with Nabila, she told him that she would help.

He didn't know if he should believe her at first—it was hard to tell what was real with all the painkillers—but then she said she'd take care of the plan. It would be just like them surviving in the garden, he thought, with her explaining how to make dinner and build shelter and if he followed all the instructions they'd be okay. She cared about him enough that she was ready to come help him. When Matthew realized this, he started to cry.

His leg was weak but now he knew he needed to get out of bed and start walking again. Soon it wasn't that bad, and he could almost walk at a normal pace with his cane. Then he needed his cane less and less. Then he didn't need his cane at all. His leg was still weak and he limped a bit, but he could move.

The next time he got access to his phone he texted Nabila that his leg was better, and she seemed so happy. It made Matthew happy. Nabila said it was time for them to put the plan into action. She had already solved the passport problem, and she was going to come meet him once he got away from the group. She told Matthew that he should stash away some food when he could, just so he'd have something to eat on the trip. Then he could leave in the middle of the night and walk until he hit the main road he'd come in on. Eventually there would be somebody driving a car or truck who would agree to take him toward Berlin.

Nabila told him that she was buying a plane ticket and would be in the city in a couple of days. She knew it might take Matthew a day or two to plan his escape and another couple to get to Berlin, but she'd be waiting when he arrived. If he could somehow keep his cellphone, then they could keep texting the whole time. If not, she told Matthew he should go to a library or internet café when he got to the city and send her an email. Then they could figure out where to meet.

Matthew was so relieved. She'd thought of everything. He texted back and said he'd follow her plan and he was excited to see her in a few days.

He tried to keep his phone after that, but they didn't let him. They said there were no exceptions, even if he was still in medical. So Matthew turned it off and put it back in the box. The next time he talked to Nabila would have to be in Berlin.

A day later, after changing the bandage on his leg, the doctor told him he had to go to the general's office for a meeting. Matthew didn't know what to think. He walked over to the general's house slowly and listened to the other men doing drills. He remembered that none of the other men liked him, and if Tom saw him, maybe he would start laughing. Matthew didn't like being so funny.

There was now a thin scab on his leg, a dark-red skin stain that would soon scar. Another day or so and he wouldn't even need a bandage.

He'd never been in the general's office before. He worried they had figured out he was planning an escape. Or maybe they were calling him in to dismiss him. Matthew was nervous.

The general sat behind a big wooden desk. He had a moustache and wore an old green army jacket, though there were no markings from any specific army. On the wall behind him were three guns, mounted on hooks. There was a stuffed eagle on a shelf in the corner.

"The man of the hour," the general boomed when Matthew walked in.

Matthew stood there for a moment, not sure what to do. He tried to think through the fog of painkillers. Then he saluted. The general chuckled. He reached out and shook Matthew's hand.

"How's the leg?"

"All good, sir."

"Good. That's very good. Here, sit down," he said, pointing to a chair in front of his desk.

The general didn't go back to his chair, though. Instead, he leaned against the desk, only a couple of feet away from Matthew, and looked down at him sitting there.

The general wasn't much older than him, Matthew guessed. It was the first time he was seeing him up close and it was hard to get a good look at his face behind the moustache, but he looked pretty young. He had a smattering of acne across his chin. But his expression was hard, his eyes unblinking.

Matthew clasped his hands in his lap. His ears were ringing because the other men had been shooting up the trees all afternoon. He was used to his hearing going in and out now, used to the constant background ringing sound that meant sometimes no real sound could get through.

"I know you've gone through quite an ordeal," the general said, "but I can see that you're recovering. And that you're dedicated to our cause."

His voice wasn't as deep as Matthew expected. He looked strong though, his shoulder muscles stretching out away from his body. Matthew nodded.

The general stared at his face, and Matthew looked back for a moment but then looked away. He wondered if he should say something else, but he didn't know what else there was to say. He tried to think of words that would work.

"We need someone for a special assignment," the general said. "You may not be able to complete regular training now, but this is a way for you to still contribute. AJ told me you'd be good for the job. Should I take his word for it?"

Matthew sat up a bit straighter. "AJ said that?" he said.

The general nodded.

"Then yes," Matthew said.

"It's not an easy assignment," the general went on. "Not everyone would be up for it." He leaned down so he was at the same level as Matthew, looked him in the eye. "But I can see you still want to contribute, soldier. This is a way you can."

Matthew stared back. He tried to keep his face calm, make sure he didn't blink too much. He was confused inside. He thought they were going to send him away, had thought that Nabila would be his only hope. But all of a sudden there was this other option. And AJ had been thinking about him, even believed he was good for an assignment. He wanted to show AJ that he was right to believe in him.

"It'll be dangerous," the general said. "But I think you can do it."

"I'm up for it," Matthew said.

The general smiled. Then he stood up and walked behind the desk, where he took a seat. He put his elbows on the desk and brought his fingers together in a triangle.

"What do you need me to do?"

The general smiled again. "I want to send you on a mission."

Matthew nodded. A few minutes ago, he was convinced they had no use for him, that he needed Nabila to help him get home. But maybe now there was another option. The ringing in his ears increased, and for a moment, he couldn't hear anything. The general was saying something else. What kind of mission? Matthew thought. It was a big deal to get sent out on your own. He tried to push aside the fuzz in his brain to focus on the general's words.

"You'd have to leave us." His hearing was back. "Like I said, you have to be ready for some danger."

Was it because of AJ's recommendation? Was that why he was chosen for the mission? Maybe AJ would send him a message again after the mission. Matthew was happy but also confused. He couldn't think straight.

"You already know that sometimes soldiers have to make sacrifices," the general went on. "Sometimes they're necessary. The good of the group is always more important than an individual."

Matthew didn't understand. "What's the mission?"

The brain fog was clearing a bit but the pain in his leg was starting to come back. He rubbed his scab with both hands.

"Does it hurt? Here, we'll take care of that."

The general opened up a drawer and put a container of pills on the table. He unscrewed the lid.

"Most people don't know who we are yet," the general said. "We're standing up to a society that has shunned us, so they need to realize what we're capable of. They need to realize that we're the ones in charge." He shook out two pills, then closed the lid. He held the pills in his hand and looked up at Matthew. "Now's the time to put all your weapons practice into action."

"What do you mean?"

The general held out the pills, and Matthew opened his fingers.

"You're going to help us get revenge," he said.

He dropped the pills into Matthew's palm, then leaned in toward Matthew's face.

"We need to show we're powerful. A force they have to pay attention to. And the best way to do that is to scare them."

Matthew froze. The pills were halfway to his mouth, but something inside him was screaming, telling him to wake up now, pay attention. "What do you mean?" he whispered.

"You're going to show them that we have control."

Matthew just stared at him. He knew they were training with guns for a reason, but the idea of shooting at anything but a tree terrified him. He could feel his arms starting to shake.

"Take your pills, son. You need to be steady."

Matthew looked down at the pills. He popped them in his mouth, swallowed hard. He wanted to be part of the group, wanted to make AJ proud, but he couldn't do this. He just couldn't. "Can I have a different mission?" he asked quietly.

"This is what we need you to do."

"I don't want to shoot people." Matthew couldn't look at him. He stared down at his hands.

"I thought you believed in our cause," the general said. He leaned back in his chair and shook his head. He let out a long sigh. "AJ thought so highly of you. That's why we chose you. I'll have to tell him you're not the man he thought you were."

Matthew could feel tears prick his eyes. He blinked fast to push them away.

"Are you really ready to give up that easily?"

Matthew looked up and saw the general stroking his chin. Saying no to the mission made him feel weak, and he hated feeling weak. The whole point of being in the group was that they were powerful. If he didn't do this, he'd throw all that away. And AJ would be so disappointed. He might never talk to Matthew again.

But what would Nabila think? She trusted him. She was helping him escape. She was coming to Berlin.

"I don't know what to do," he said.

The general pushed his chair back and stood up. He walked around the desk and leaned on the edge again. He was closer now and Matthew could smell his breath.

"You can choose not to," the general said. He shrugged. "We'll just get one of the other men to do the mission." He tapped his fingers on the desk. "But you should know," he said, "that if you're not ready to do something like this, there's no point in us training you. There's no point in keeping you around."

Matthew looked up at him, then looked away. He was trying to figure out what the general was saying but it was still hard to think.

"We could make an example of you," he continued. "Show the rest of the group that this is what happens when you betray the brother-hood, when you let a woman take control of you."

Matthew snapped up.

"You think we aren't checking in on you?" The general chuckled. "We've seen every message you've sent to your precious Nabila. She'd be easy to find if we wanted to find her."

Matthew couldn't move. He still couldn't think straight but he knew that things were suddenly very bad. This wasn't supposed to happen.

The general leaned toward him. "This is your last chance," he said. "You've worked so hard. Do you really want to give all that up?"

Matthew's chest was hurting.

"So?"

The general was still staring at him. He rubbed his moustache. "So? Do you accept this mission?"

Matthew didn't want to do it. He didn't even think he could do it. But this was his chance to be powerful, to live up to AJ's expectations. And they knew about Nabila.

"Yes," Matthew whispered.

"Good," the general said. "We'll get things ready."

He got up from the table, and Matthew knew he was supposed to get up too, but he couldn't move. Instead he just sat there and stared at his fingers.

M atthew thinks they won't play on the roof when a lot of snow comes, but that's when Nabila likes the stillness of things. Everything is quieter in the winter, she tells him, when ice on the garden wall shines in the sunlight, when the snow covers each individual leaf of each plant. "You can't hear too many noises of the city, not when there's frost in the air," she tells him as they dig through the snow. "It's as if all the streetcars and taxis are very far away."

Matthew gets cold easily, so Nabila digs out a little spot for him behind the rose bush where he'll be protected from the wind. She also lends him her mittens. His own mittens have holes in the thumbs, and the skin that sticks out when he wears them is always bright red.

The sun sets early at this time of year, and Nabila makes up different reasons for the approaching darkness. There are earthquakes happening, and the new mountains forming are getting tall enough to block the light. Or an asteroid has hit the earth and is flinging tons of dirt into the air. It's getting stuck bit by bit in the atmosphere, and will eventually cover the sunlight.

Matthew isn't sure about those ideas, but he doesn't ask many questions because he's too preoccupied with keeping his hands warm. He doesn't have a proper hat either, just a hood on his jacket, and Nabila says that he is going to catch a cold.

Sure enough, the next week Matthew is sick and doesn't come to school for a few days. Tara Lynn speaks to his teacher, and then they ask Nabila to pick up his homework. She doesn't really want to, knows she'd have to wait until everyone else from her class has left the school building, but then she finds out that Matthew's sisters will be the ones picking it up from her, the same way they pick Matthew up from her apartment building. She'll get to go downstairs and meet them in the lobby to hand it over.

After school his teacher gives her a blue folder with photocopied pages of math and spelling homework, and Nabila carries it in front of her all the way home, rifling through the pages that Matthew has to do. There isn't a lot of work, but she knows it will take him a long time. He probably won't even finish all of it.

She plays on her own in their forest. Her mother told her that sometimes seawater freezes too, just at a lower temperature, so she imagines parts of the streets around the building covered in ice, whales bumping up against it to try to break through. She breaks twigs into small pieces and mixes it with snow. She makes sealant to waterproof their shelter and a stew that will keep them warm.

When Matthew's sisters arrive, Tara Lynn says she can go downstairs to the lobby alone if she comes right back up. Nabila grabs the blue folder and runs down.

Roxanne and Libby are wearing sneakers even though there is snow on the ground. Their jeans trail on the floor and are wet halfway to their knees. "Aren't your feet cold?" Nabila asks. They say no.

She doesn't want to give them the folder right away. She wants to know if Libby still likes that guitar player from the high school band, if Roxanne is going to dye her hair pink again when the colour all grows out. Libby snaps her gum and says, "Yeah." Roxanne says she doesn't know.

"Are you gonna give us the homework, or do you want to keep it?" Roxanne says then. Libby laughs. Nabila feels a bit embarrassed. She doesn't let go of the folder, though. She has another question she wants to ask.

"Your dad's not actually a soldier, right?" she says.

Libby stops laughing. She rolls her eyes at Nabila. "Are you gonna give us the homework or not?"

"So where is he if he's not a solider?"

"Who the hell knows?"

Libby snaps her gum again and crosses her arms. Roxanne puts one hand on her hip, and the other hand out for the homework. Nabila holds on to it.

"Why doesn't he live with you anymore?"

"You know, you're a nosy kid."

Nabila feels her face grow hot.

Roxanne clears her throat, sticks her hand out again. "Homework?"

"What did he do?"

"It doesn't matter," Roxanne says.

Libby blows air out of her mouth and her bangs fly up. "He used to hit us. And Mom."

"Libby!"

"She wanted to know."

"You'll scare her."

"He used to knock us around like we were pieces of meat."

"Seriously. She's a little kid."

Nabila watches as they look at each other, Roxanne frowning, Libby blowing a purple bubble with her gum. Something inside Nabila starts to hurt.

"One time he picked me up and threw me against the wall and I had to go to the hospital," Libby says.

"Okay. That's enough. We're going." Roxanne grabs her sister's arm and pulls her toward the door. Libby flips her hair and lets herself be led away.

It is only after they leave, once they disappear down the sidewalk, that Nabila realizes she is still holding Matthew's homework. She knows she can't go back upstairs with it. On her way to the elevator, she drops the folder down the garbage chute.

That evening, Nabila doesn't want dinner. The house smells of frying lamb, of ginger and warm bread, and every time she thinks about the food her stomach tightens. She wonders about Matthew, wonders if he is lying in bed or watching TV, unaware of his math and spelling and the fact that his father is a horrible person. When her own father comes home from work, he holds her up against him and she thinks about how small she is, how easy it would be for him to hold her down or throw her around. How she wouldn't be able to stop it.

At the dinner table, she tells her parents she isn't feeling well. They want her to try to eat anyway. When her father puts a piece of lamb on her plate, she can feel her heart start to pound against the weight of Matthew's secret. She can feel it now locked inside her chest.

He liked to think that Nabila was picturing him travelling, was imagining a truck with him hiding in the back flatbed, him running across a border, him fighting through mud and crawling beneath a razor-wire fence. The reality was that they were just sending him off, but he knew that Nabila wasn't aware of that. She might think he was brave for sneaking out, for standing up to them. He didn't want to ruin that.

He had no way of telling Nabila about the mission. Even if he had his phone, he didn't know what to say to her, and he didn't know what he was going to do. He wondered if he could sneak off and follow Nabila's plan instead, but he didn't know if they'd be watching him. It was all a muddled problem and Matthew hadn't figured out a way to sort things out.

There had been a small send-off when he left, a little announcement at the last meeting explaining that he was going on a mission. They'd hear about his work soon. There was a bit of banging on the tables but then someone snickered, and any pride Matthew had felt melted away.

Matthew wasn't allowed to take his duffle bag or most of his things, because they said he wouldn't be needing them. Instead, they gave him a large backpack. It was the kind that people carried if they were travelling from hostel to hostel for months on end, and he wasn't supposed to let it out of his sight. It was long enough to hold the rifle they'd given him. The gun was the most important thing, they'd said, and he had to keep it concealed until it was time to use it. He also had some food and a blue tarp because they told him he'd have to camp in the forest to avoid suspicion.

He'd had a practice session with the gun the day before. He'd never fired anything that let off so many rounds so fast, and afterwards his shoulder was sore. A bunch of the bullets had hit the trees, though. He felt awful, terrified, but also proud because some of the men had come out to watch him shoot and had hollered with the gunfire.

The general wouldn't give him back his phone. Matthew had asked for it, but the general said it was a privilege, and he had to earn it. Maybe if he followed orders, he'd said, but Matthew would have to prove himself first. Until then, someone else would be in charge.

That person turned out to be Tom, since he was driving Matthew back to Berlin. Matthew watched as the general handed his phone over to Tom, who put it in his pocket. As they were getting into the truck Tom clapped him on the shoulder, said they were going to have fun.

Matthew felt lost. He settled into his seat and stared out the window, tried not to look at Tom. They pulled away from headquarters and onto the road. Then it was just the two of them.

Tom was smoking a cigarette and kept blowing smoke in Matthew's direction, making him cough. He put on loud music.

"I called it from the start," he shouted over at Matthew.

Matthew didn't say anything. He just stared straight ahead at the road, watched the motorcycle that was in front of them. He had no energy for Tom. The drive was only a few hours, he knew, just a few hours until he would be rid of him.

Tom sat back in his seat and looked over at him. He smirked. "I knew you were scared. Didn't I say that? Could see it in you right away. Could smell it." He cackled. "You're still scared."

Matthew stared at the road.

"I heard you were telling your little girlfriend all about us." He blew smoke out his mouth and for a moment it filled the front seat. "That true? Hey, that true?"

Matthew didn't want to look at Tom.

"The bigger question is, how the fuck did you get a girlfriend?" Tom laughed, and it was meaner than usual. Matthew rubbed his leg. He was worried about the mission, and about Nabila, and now about being alone with Tom. He didn't like any of this.

"Holy shit she must have been desperate." Tom took another drag of his cigarette. "I can't fucking believe it. Is she ugly? Hey, look at me. Hey. I bet she's ugly."

"She's beautiful," Matthew whispered to the dashboard.

"What?"

"Stop talking about her!" Matthew's leg was hurting, and his voice had come out louder than he'd expected. Out of the corner of his eye, he saw Tom jump in surprise. But then he regained his composure, leaned toward Matthew and dropped ash from the cigarette into his lap. Matthew's leg jerked and he brushed it off with his hand. It left a grey streak.

"You're such a loser," Tom said. "Fuck. You actually have a girl-friend?" he shook his head and laughed, and Matthew was going to say she wasn't actually his girlfriend, but he realized it didn't matter. And then he realized that Tom was jealous.

His leg was starting to throb again. He reached into his pocket, took out a couple of pills and popped them in his mouth.

"You're gonna be a fucking addict," Tom said. He finished his ciga-rette and threw the butt out the window. They were driving past fields with dead crops, brown and dark yellow and washed-out grey.

Tom looked back over at Matthew. He smirked. "Wanna hear a secret?"

Matthew just wanted him to stop talking. He didn't say anything.

"That accident with your leg? Well. It wasn't an accident."

Matthew's head jerked up and Tom started laughing. He was watch-ing Matthew more than he was watching the road now. Matthew was trying to make sense of what he was hearing but his brain was working slowly. The pills hadn't kicked in yet and everything still felt foggy and unsure.

"But we're on the same side," Matthew whispered.

"What?"

"Why?" Matthew said a bit louder.

"Because you're not one of us," Tom said. He was banging the steer-ing wheel to the beat of the radio and Matthew could see the dashboard vibrate. "At least they found some use for you." He started laughing again and it hurt Matthew's head.

He just wanted to be in Berlin. Where Nabila was supposed to meet him. Maybe she was already there. There was too much to think about; Matthew needed some air and he needed some peace.

"Can we stop for a bathroom break?"

"What?"

"A bathroom break!"

"Shit, what are you, seven? You can't hold it?"

"Just two minutes."

For a moment Matthew thought he wasn't going to stop, but then he felt the truck slowing down. Tom pulled onto the shoulder and turned off the engine. The radio stopped. Matthew exhaled slowly.

"You taking a leak or what? We don't got all day."

Matthew pushed open the door and got out of the truck. It was starting to get dark, and he could hear the wind coming across the dead field. He took a few steps toward the old plants.

The quiet of the evening made him breathe a bit easier. His mind was less foggy, and then he knew he was scared of dying. A while ago, when he was stuck at headquarters, he thought it might not be so bad, but now he wondered if it was going to hurt. He worried that it was going to be so much worse than the pain in his leg and last so much longer. Then he hated that he was only worried about the pain. He wished he had more energy.

Matthew didn't really have to go, but he knew Tom would yell at him if he didn't. So he unzipped his pants and peed onto the crumpled plants in front of him. His back was to the truck, but he could hear Tom get out of the other door, walk around toward the front of the cab. Matthew finished quickly, zipped himself back up.

When he turned around Tom was watching him. He'd lit another cigarette and the end of it was glowing orange in the low evening light. He was leaning against the truck, his other hand in his pocket.

"While you're busy with your mission," he said slowly, "maybe I'll go find your girlfriend." He took another drag on the cigarette and didn't take his eyes off Matthew. "You know. Keep her company."

The air was suddenly very cold around Matthew. He thought of Nabila, of her long hair, of Tom watching her from far away and then coming up behind her. The thought of her being scared terrified him. He could feel adrenaline running through his arms, his fingers. He realized he was angry.

Matthew hated Tom. Matthew had always hated Tom, but now he was talking about Nabila. He couldn't let him talk about Nabila.

Tom was still staring at Matthew. The glowing ember at the end of the cigarette lit up the corner of his jawline. "What she look like?" he said.

Matthew yelled. He rushed at Tom with his arms out, and caught the surprise in his eyes before he barrelled into him. He stuck his elbows out and slammed Tom back in the truck and heard his body hit it hard. Then he hit him into the truck again. Tom's hand was still in his pocket, and he was calling for Matthew to stop, but he didn't. He rammed his elbow into Tom's face.

There was a cracking sound and Tom shouted and then Matthew hit him again. He'd never seen fear in Tom before. He was punching him now, in his face, in his stomach. He would not let Tom anywhere near Nabila.

"You stay away from her!" he heard himself scream. It felt loud. He was still punching Tom, who was stuck between Matthew and the cab. "Stay away from her!"

"Okay, okay!" Tom was trying to cover his head with his hand. "It was just a joke. I promise. I promise, okay?"

Matthew didn't stop. There was blood now on his hands, blood coming from somewhere on Tom's face. It looked velvet black in the near darkness. Tom was saying stop, stop, over and over again, and Matthew had never felt this strong.

"I'll leave her alone!" Tom screamed. "I don't even know who the fuck she is. Please, man."

Matthew kept hitting him until Tom slumped down beside the front wheel. Then he took a step back, caught his breath. His hands were bloody and so was the front of Tom's shirt. He was so angry. He thought maybe he could have killed him if he kept going. Matthew had never felt that before.

He clenched his fists, but he let Tom get up, steady himself against the front of the truck. Matthew took a step toward him and watched as Tom's entire body tensed right up. He was scared now, Matthew realized. Tom was scared of him.

"Let's just get back in the car, okay man? Let's just drive," Tom said.

Matthew nodded. His heart was still pounding, and it felt like he could barely contain himself, like all the anger and sadness and power was trying to burst through his skin. He walked around to the other side of the truck and got in. Tom got behind the wheel.

"No more jokes," Matthew said.

"Yeah, whatever man. Let's just drive."

He started the car and the radio began blasting but Matthew turned it off. Tom didn't stop him. Matthew stared out the window at the dark fields and didn't know what he was going to do.

Tom drove without talking to Matthew after that, which suited Matthew just fine. It was dark when they entered the city. They drove past buildings and shops and houses, and then Tom stopped the truck on a quiet street next to a wooded area.

"Now we wait," Tom said.

His voice sounded strange after so much silence. Matthew looked at him. "For what?"

Tom glanced over in his direction. Matthew saw that his nose was at an odd angle. There was dried blood along his cheek and down his neck. "Your bodyguard," Tom said. "I'm not sticking around to be your fucking babysitter."

Matthew forced himself to try and think clearly. He didn't know what he'd expected, but with a bodyguard he wouldn't be able to get away to email Nabila. And Tom still had his phone. He didn't know if it was a good idea to tell Nabila where he was or not. He didn't want her to show up there, but he also worried that he would die and not even Nabila would have any idea what had happened. And she was waiting for a message from him.

"Can I have my phone back?" Matthew asked.

Tom laughed.

But now Matthew wasn't scared of Tom. He was still laughing with his mouth wide open when Matthew lunged across the front seat at him, slammed his elbow into his jaw. The laughter turned to a howl of pain. Tom was so used to being in control, thought Matthew. It was so easy to catch him off guard.

Matthew stuck his hands into Tom's jacket pocket where he'd seen him stash the phone hours ago. It took a bit of wriggling, some elbows to Tom's already sore ribs, and then Matthew had it in his hand.

He jumped out of the car and turned on the phone. It was raining and Tom was shouting something at him, but Matthew wasn't listening. He figured he didn't have much time.

A flood of notifications from Nabila popped up on the phone. She was here, in the same city. And she'd been wondering what was happening.

Matthew heard the truck door open and slam, so he ran up the street a bit, hobbling on his weak leg. I'm in Berlin, he messaged Nabila as he went. He had no idea what part of the city he was in, but there was an intersection up ahead with some streetlights and signs. I can't see you yet, he wrote. He made it to the intersection and took a picture of the street signs, said he was camping nearby. He sent the message and the photo, then started another one to tell her that things might be dangerous and that he didn't know if he would be able to get away anymore. That's when a fist hit him in the back of the head.

Matthew's knees hit the pavement. His head was in agony and so were his legs. He heard himself cry out.

There was a man standing beside him now. He was tall with a massive chest, and had hands nearly the size of soccer balls. He bent down and pried the phone out of Matthew's fingers. Matthew tried to hold on but he couldn't do anything. There was no way he could get the upper hand with this man the way he had with Tom. He was just too big.

The man tucked the phone into a pocket inside his coat. "No more texting," he said.

It was difficult for Matthew to stand up. His thigh was sore and now his knees were sore, and the back of his head was still throbbing. The man stuck out an arm and Matthew didn't want to take it, but he had no choice. He reached out and the man helped him up.

He heard Tom snickering. "You're already getting along with your new bodyguard," he said. Matthew looked at him. He was standing a bit farther back, but he could see the blood on Tom's neck and shirt starting to run in the rain.

"He's got a girlfriend he's texting," Tom said to the bodyguard.

The big man grunted. "I know."

Tom disappeared for a moment, and Matthew thought he was gone, but then he reappeared with the backpack. He left it on the ground next to Matthew's feet.

Matthew wanted to scream, to make someone listen to him. He was soaked with rain and his body hurt and he didn't want to be here. But he didn't know what he could do.

And then Tom was really gone. Matthew heard the truck engine start and then the truck drove away. He and the bodyguard both waited until the sound faded and all they could hear was rain again. Matthew looked up at the man's face. It was like a brick wall.

"Get moving," he said, and Matthew reached down for his back-pack. The bodyguard took two flashlights out of his jacket and held one out to Matthew. "It's a bit of a walk," he said. "I hope you're not scared of the forest."

When it started to rain, Nabila found a spot on the sidewalk beneath the overhang of a shoe shop. She stood there for nearly half an hour, watching the water run along the concrete. She thought about walking out into it because she usually enjoyed the rain, but she was feeling a bit fragile in this strange city, and knew that getting wet wouldn't help. So instead she waited there and wrapped her jacket tight around her body. The overhang didn't keep away the cold, though. By the time the rain had subsided, she was shivering and her shoes were soaked.

It was almost dark by the time she made her way back to Café Arboretum. She found Tierney alone in the front room, watering the plants.

"Girl, get in here! You look freezing."

Tierney put down the watering can and pulled out a chair with red cushions close to the counter. Nabila didn't have the energy to protest. She sank into the seat, and Tierney rushed behind the espresso bar, started steaming milk. Nabila could hear the liquid bubbling.

"It's going to rain all night, I was listening to the weather. It's more rain than we've had in months." Tierney reached over and grabbed a mug that was so wide it could have been a bowl. "The neighbours are worried about drainage, but they're always worried about drainage here. I don't know why."

"Because the ground is already so saturated," Nabila said.

"What?"

"Never mind."

She pulled her hands up into her sleeves, but then realized that her jacket was still pretty wet. She took it off and hung it over another chair, then got up and walked over to one of the bookcases, ran her fingers over the waxy leaves of a succulent. She no longer wanted to be upset

139

with Tierney, not when Matthew was still silent, when she was supposed to see him in just a couple of days and hand over the thing that would save him, that would finally rescue him from the mistake he'd gotten caught up in. In relation to all that, the fight with Tierney didn't really matter.

"Here, you're going to love this," Tierney said. She was pouring things behind the bar, then shaking a can of whipped cream. "It's one of our specialties. Hot chocolate with a bit of chili, a bit of spice. It'll warm you right up."

Nabila sat back down and Tierney presented her with the mug. There was a leaf design poured into the milk foam on the right-hand side, a tower of whipped cream on the other with a sprinkling of brown dust on top. She stuck her finger in to taste it.

"Cinnamon? On hot chocolate?"

"Just try it."

It was delicious. The milk was sweet and hot, and she felt her body calming, begin to warm. Tierney went back to watering the plants, and Nabila watched her as she moved around the room, humming to herself, sometimes dancing to the song in her head. Outside, it started to rain again. People rushed by the windows with umbrellas or newspapers held over their hair, but inside the radiator in the corner was cranked up. Nabila could see ripples of heat rising above it.

She'd taken her phone out of her pocket and had left it sitting on the table, so when it buzzed, the sound reverberated across the wood. It made Tierney jump.

"Jesus. And that's with the actual ringer off? How loud is that thing?"

But Nabila wasn't listening. A text had just come through. It was a message from Matthew.

She exhaled slowly, opened it up. It said that he was in Berlin. He couldn't see her yet, though. He was camping near a specific intersection.

"Nabila? Everything okay?"

"Yeah." She took another deep breath. She didn't understand why she couldn't just give him his passport today.

"Are you sure?"

She looked up, saw Tierney watching her.

"It's fine," she said. She read over the message again, glanced at the picture he'd sent with it. "It's my boyfriend actually, who I was telling you about. He's in the city."

"Oh?"

"Yeah. He just got here."

"Okay. Is he going to stay with you upstairs?"

"No," Nabila said, then realized that her answer had come too forcefully and too quickly. "I mean, he's pitching a tent," she amended. "That's how he usually travels. Somewhere in the woods I guess."

"Really? Okay. Huh."

She realized how ridiculous it all sounded. But she usually needed time to prepare her lies, and she'd been caught off guard, didn't understand why he was camping. Maybe there were people looking for him and he needed to stay off the radar, but he hadn't mentioned it, hadn't said anything to suggest it. And it would be miserable with all the rain tonight.

"So, are you going to stay with him?" Tierney asked.

"Uh, no," Nabila said. She took a long sip of her hot chocolate. "Not when I've got this room here."

Tierney went back to the plants, but she glanced over at Nabila, a slight frown on her face. Nabila took another drink of hot chocolate. "It's just," she started again, trying to figure out what to say. "He's just been gone for a while."

"Oh, okay." Tierney nodded. "I got it." She wiped up a drop of water she'd spilled on the floor. "You're waiting to see where things stand? Where you two are at?"

"Yeah."

"Got it." She made her way along the far wall of the room, pulling plants out from between books and then putting them back. "That makes sense. Don't worry about it. You guys will figure things out when you see each other." She went back behind the counter, refilled the watering can. "Things are always easier in person."

"Right," Nabila said.

Tierney finished her loop of the room, then went through the door behind the counter and returned without the watering can. She switched on some music. Out the window, it was pouring. Nabila imagined the war tree swaying in the wind, the water droplets pounding against the yellow leaves. She'd assumed they would talk as soon as he arrived. That he could explain things a bit more. And didn't he want his passport as soon as he could get it?

"So, are we just ignoring him?" Tierney said.

Nabila looked up.

"I mean, you will see him before you fly home, right?"

"I sure hope so."

"Okay."

Nabila rested her elbows against the table, cradled her forehead in her hands. She tried to relax her shoulders.

"I mean, I'd like to see him today," she said. She didn't want to share too much with Tierney, but everything was starting to feel strange and she needed to talk it out. "It's just, in his text he didn't suggest it. He said we can't meet up yet."

Tierney put down the plate she'd been drying. She leaned against the counter, crossed her arms. "Now I see. This is coming from him."

Nabila shrugged.

"You flew all this way, came to a city you didn't know, and now he doesn't want to see you. What a jackass."

Nabila looked down at the table. Things had been tenuous to begin with, but now she didn't understand at all what was going on, as if the strings holding it together no longer had any give. It felt like everything might snap apart. She had the passport just upstairs. She'd feel better once it was handed over.

"Nabila? Don't worry. We're going to make this work." Tierney flung the tea towel that she was still holding over her head, let it come to rest over her shoulder. "We'll make him talk to you tonight. We'll go somewhere close to where he is, give him no option."

"How?"

"Do you know where he's camping?"

Nabila looked down at her phone and pulled up his message again, then tapped on the photo that Matthew had sent with it. She turned the screen to Tierney and pointed at the intersection. "Know where that is?"

Tierney nodded. "Oh yeah," she said. "There's a stretch of forest near there where people always squat."

"How do you know that?"

"I've been there before. The police don't go there that often, so it's kind of a rough area. I hope he knows what he's doing."

Nabila took her elbows off the table and sat up straight. "How rough?"

"The usual riff-raff. Hey, he's not a criminal is he? Is that why he's there?"

Nabila shook her head, but she was starting to wonder.

"Never mind. Not relevant. But this is good, right? We'll pick a place nearby, get him to come meet you. Then at least you'll know one way or another."

Tierney was making plans fast. Nabila tried to figure out what would make the most sense, but Tierney was already scrolling through her phone, assessing options. "I know where we're going," she said, raising her hand in the air. "There's this great place near that area, and every once in a while the train runs right by, you can see it from inside the bar real close. My DJ plays there most nights, he'll get us in. Your guy, too."

"What do you mean the train runs right by? And I want to talk with Matthew, not dance."

"There's a quieter section, too. And a patio. You'll be able to talk with your Matthew. And then I can dance with my DJ." Tierney grinned, clasped her hands together.

Nabila rubbed her forehead. "Okay," she said slowly. "I guess that could work."

"Of course it will work!" Tierney was dancing behind the espresso bar now, her movements much faster than the music they had playing. "You just have to tell him now. Here, this is the address. Tell him we can get in free."

Nabila wasn't sure about it. She picked up her phone, but didn't reply to Matthew's message yet. She needed some time to think. She felt uneasy about the way things were happening.

Tierney continued drying the dishes, and Nabila went upstairs and removed her soggy socks. Then she took a shower. She stood under the hot water and listened to the rain on the roof, tried to figure out where things had started to go sideways. Nothing had changed, really, she'd still just hand over the passport and be done with it. But she couldn't get rid of the feeling that everything had started to turn.

The rain slowed to a drizzle in the evening, and the café became busy. Tierney ran around serving lattes and croissants, wiping tables, and Nabila stood in a quiet corner of the room, going through the bookshelf. She picked up any interesting titles, read the back cover, then returned them to their place. She was trying to keep her mind busy. She didn't want to think about other things.

She finally decided to go with Tierney's plan. She hadn't been able to come up with anything else, and if she did see him tonight, she could hand over the passport. She wrote back to him that she was glad he was in Berlin, and that she wanted to see him. That she'd brought what he'd asked for, and it would be good to chat in person after so long. She told him where to meet her, and at what time. She even gave him some directions.

Matthew didn't respond. He'd changed since going away, she realized. She just didn't know how different he would be.

She remembered when she'd first introduced him to the idea that the garden on the top of her building was a forest. He hadn't been able to grasp it until she'd made him close his eyes and picture trees with long roots crawling down the exterior walls, picture everyone else except for the two of them either dead or gone away. It had scared him, but he wasn't allowed to open his eyes, she told him, until he believed it. When he finally did, she could see that something had set. That he'd convinced himself better than she ever could.

By the time Tierney closed the café, the rain had picked up again. It wasn't a great night to go out, she said, but it would be good for Matthew, since his other option was lying in the wet woods. She went into the kitchen and came out with two glasses of fruit juice mixed with vodka, handed one to Nabila. Nabila was ready to go, but Tierney said she still needed some time to get ready. So Nabila sat in her bedroom, flipping through a book she'd borrowed from downstairs, while Tierney stood in front of the mirror in the bathroom and rubbed powder into her cheeks and over her eyes.

She wondered if Matthew would just not respond and not show up. A few hours ago she would have said that was impossible, but as the time ticked on, she began to consider it. It made her angry, because she was here to do a favour for him. She could very well just refuse to help him out, she thought, and maybe she should threaten to, but she didn't really think that would accomplish anything. Still, Matthew needed to understand that if she was going to help him, she needed some assurances. She needed to hear things from his perspective, and needed to know where he'd been and what he'd been doing. The first thing she wanted to know was why he was squatting in the woods like a fugitive.

Nabila picked up her phone and sent him another message. For months she'd been wary of being too harsh with him, but now she didn't care as much, thought maybe he should hear her upset. She told him that she expected him to be there. That she'd be waiting by the main bar.

Down the hall, Tierney was blasting German pop. Nabila could tell that she was singing along by imitating just the sounds, falling short of stringing together German words.

She would have never chosen a bar to meet Matthew, but the idea was starting to grow on her. If he was in trouble, if he was being followed by someone, it would be easier to blend into the crowd. She didn't want to get caught up in anything larger than simply helping him get home.

Tierney turned off the music and came down the hall, stuck her head through the open door.

"Ready to go?"

Nabila put the book down. She had Matthew's passport tucked away in her purse. Out in the hallway, Tierney had on purple eye-shadow, her lashes thick and long enough to touch her cheeks when she blinked. There were sparkles on the edge of her eyes that matched her tooth diamond.

They walked out into the rain huddled under a single umbrella. Nabila had looked up a map this time, knew exactly which train they were taking and where they were going. She wasn't about to let Tierney run the logistics again. Tierney was a good talker, though, and Nabila remembered that she did enjoy her company, liked listening to her talk about book shipments and the plants in her summer garden. She had no trouble saying exactly what she was thinking, Nabila realized. Nabila wasn't so used to people who didn't hold things back.

By the time they got to the S-Bahn, Tierney had started telling her about her DJ. That was how she referred to him, always with possession, and Nabila found it funny but she didn't let it show. Tierney had met him in line at the grocery store, she said, and he'd invited her out to a show. After he'd finished his set the two of them had danced for hours and then had gone up to the club's roof and watched the sun come up. After that, she hadn't seen him for five weeks. Until she finally went to another one of his shows, and they'd done it all over again.

The train took a while and Tierney continued to talk. She told Nabila how she wouldn't abandon her tonight, no matter how good things went with her DJ. "Nothing like last night, I promise," she said, with a rather stoic expression. "Unless you want to go off with Matthew, of course. Then you just let me know." Tierney winked, and laughed, and her sparkles reflected the light.

Nabila hadn't told her that Matthew hadn't confirmed. Tierney hadn't asked, so Nabila had just stayed quiet, pretended like everything was normal. But she wondered.

They got off at the end of the line and exited the station. It was dark enough to be the middle of the night. Tierney led her along the sidewalk, and Nabila tried to picture the directions she'd looked up, tried to understand exactly where they were going. There weren't a lot of people around, though there were streetlights shining spheres of illumination along the road ahead. It was still raining. Her shoes were wet again. Then they cut down a side street and Nabila could feel the faint thump of music, of bass and drums and synthesizer coming from nearby.

Tierney led her around a corner and toward a doorway cut out of the wall. "We won't wait, don't worry," she said, and then Nabila noticed the small line, the group of people hovering by the entrance.

The bouncer took one look at Tierney and nodded. He stepped aside, and Tierney linked arms with Nabila and pulled her through the door. The door led to a staircase, and they climbed up a couple of storeys, and then right back down again, before it levelled out into a long dark hallway. The music was heavier now, an electronic beat that Nabila could feel in her leg bones. There were lights up ahead.

The room at the end of the hallway was already filled with people. The air was humid and warm, smelled of beer and sweat and wet clothing. There was a bar off in the corner with a small seating area away from the dance floor, a stage at the back and an exit that led onto a patio on the right. Hanging from the ceiling were lights; they were strobe lights and spotlights that swivelled back and forth, catching a wrist here, a torso there. There was white and blue and then purple, and Nabila watched as they rippled over the crowd, blended together to create a kind of turquoise. The music moved up and up and up, and then came right back down.

Tierney was saying something, laughing. She was swaying to the song, and then Nabila realized that she was swaying, too, and then they were dancing in the middle of a crowd of people. It threw her off for a moment, the idea that she was dancing in a club. But the lights were like sunshine waving through the euphotic layer of the ocean, and she put her hands in the air without thinking, spun around.

They made their way to the bar after that, got a drink. Tierney pulled her farther into the room toward the stage where there was a DJ standing behind a turntable, a baseball cap perched sideways on his head. Tierney turned toward Nabila. "Whaddaya think?" she gushed, her eyes so full of colour.

Nabila smiled and nodded, though she really couldn't get a good look at the man at all.

"Right?" Tierney squealed.

They danced on their section of floor for a few minutes, Tierney making grand gestures with her hands that Nabila realized were meant to attract attention. Nabila kept looking toward the bar on the far side, checking if she recognized anybody. She didn't see Matthew yet. A bit of anger was starting to creep up over her, though she tried to push it back down, continued to dance. If he didn't show up, she didn't think she wanted to help him.

Then the floor started to rumble. Tierney pulled on her arm. "Look!' she said, shaking her shoulder.

The train entered Nabila's field of view like a rocket. The tracks must have been just outside, and it passed right behind the bar, visible through the windows, making the liquor bottles shake. Everyone around her started cheering. There was an energy in being in the middle of the crowd, she realized, a kind of happiness that bubbled up in her throat. A man she didn't know turned around and gave her a high-five.

She was aware of the colours again, of the purple spotlight snapshotting someone's bra strap, then an arm with a lion tattoo. Someone sloshed beer over their hand and licked it off their wrist.

Tierney pulled Nabila toward her, shouted in her ear. "Where are you meeting him?" she asked.

Nabila pointed toward the bar, and Tierney downed the rest of her drink, left the glass on a railing on the side wall.

"Time to get another anyway," she said.

They held hands and weaved through the crowd. Nabila could feel the heat of bodies all around her, watched purple skin and blue hair move to the music. There was something to this, she realized. She could appreciate the lightness of the moment, the ease with which people were moving.

Matthew still wasn't at the bar. Tierney wormed through the crowd and ordered new drinks for both of them, and Nabila surveyed the people nearby, looked for pale hair and soft features. She wondered if he had gotten lost, if he was stuck on the wrong street or couldn't find the right doorway. Next to her there were only women in tank tops with shots of tequila, and a man in a mesh shirt speaking loudly to his friend in English. Behind him, there was a big man in a black jacket making eyes at her.

"I'll wait with you," Tierney said as she came back toward Nabila and handed her a drink. Nabila still hadn't finished her first one. She drank it down quickly, then left the empty glass on the bar, moved back toward Tierney. The man in the jacket was still watching her. Some foam from his beer was stuck in his stubble.

This was it, Nabila thought. If Matthew wasn't going to take on any of the responsibility, she couldn't either. She couldn't help him if he refused to see her.

In the background the music changed, but Nabila didn't really think much about it until she realize that Tierney was starting to get antsy. They'd switched to recorded tracks, she noticed then. The DJ was taking a break, and Tierney wanted to go find him.

"I'm fine," Nabila said. She looked at Tierney, then nodded toward the stage.

"Are you sure?"

"Yes. I'll be right here."

Tierney seemed to collapse with relief.

"Go get him."

She leaned in and kissed Nabila on the forehead, then started pushing through the crowd. A moment later, she was swallowed up in a sea of gyrating bodies. Nabila turned her attention to her drink, took a lengthy sip.

She stood there for a bit, browsed through her phone. The man in the jacket came up to her and asked if he could buy her a drink, but she told him she was waiting for someone, and he stomped off. A few places opened up in the seating area, and she thought about claiming a spot, but before she could get to them they were taken. She finished her drink. Matthew was supposed to book his own ticket back when he got to Berlin, but he needed his passport for that. So she didn't understand why he was avoiding her. It made her uneasy.

She ordered another cocktail and walked around the entire perimeter of the room, scanning the crowd. There were a couple of men with very light hair but they weren't Matthew. She looked for Tierney and her DJ, but she couldn't see them either. Nabila made her way back to the bar and stood there again, hoping somehow Matthew might appear. She was starting to feel very lonely. And frustrated.

Matthew wasn't coming, she realized. He would have been here by now. Suddenly she was angry.

She left the bar and made her way to the bathroom and closed herself into the stall at the end. She shut her eyes and tried to breathe slowly, pictured a seascape with blue light, with kelp waving in the water. Outside the stall door there were girls trying to clean beer off their dresses. There was someone singing loudly, her friends laughing, someone else having a conversation on a cellphone.

Nabila didn't understand what Matthew was doing. She wanted to help him, but it was like he didn't want to be helped. It didn't make sense. She pushed the hair back from her eyes and washed her face.

She didn't want to wait for Tierney. She texted her, then called a cab, stood next to the bouncer until it pulled up on the curb. The drive seemed to take a long time. When she got home, she went to bed but she couldn't sleep. Instead she switched off the light and lay there staring at the ceiling, listening to her own breathing.

The bodyguard led Matthew through the woods and the two men barely said anything. Matthew was focused on where he was stepping, because everything was muddy and slippery and he couldn't see in the dark. There was only a small circle of light from the flashlight, so he saw the forest floor in glimpses: an old leaf here, some branches over there.

It was hard to hear past the rain in the trees, but Matthew was pretty sure they passed a few other people. At one point he saw an orange tarp. Eventually the bodyguard stopped and said this was the place they would be camping. He asked Matthew if he had a tent, and Matthew took the blue tarp out of the backpack and the two of them strung it up between two trees. Matthew also had a sleeping bag that he spread out beneath the tarp.

Then the bodyguard had said he should get some rest. He had his own tarp nearby, and he'd hear if Matthew tried to go anywhere.

The bodyguard waited until Matthew was settled on the ground and then he disappeared. Matthew was cold and his body still ached. He wanted to run away, but he had nowhere to go. He didn't even know how to get back to the main road. Even though he couldn't stop shivering, eventually Matthew fell asleep. It was easier than sitting there and thinking about how awful everything seemed to have gotten.

The next morning his bodyguard came by and told Matthew that he'd seen Nabila. He'd paid her a visit the night before while Matthew had been sleeping, he said. She'd texted him exactly where to find her.

He showed Matthew a photo on his phone. It was of Nabila in a dark room full of people, a bar or a club, wearing tight jeans and a green shirt. Matthew wanted to scream and cry and punch this man all at the same time. He could send her a message anytime now from Matthew's phone, he said, and she'd be so easy to get to.

Matthew was furious with himself for not waking up, for taking painkillers and being unable to do anything. And he was angry for not protecting her. Matthew took a swing at his bodyguard then, but he just caught Matthew's fist and forced him down to the ground. Matthew couldn't do anything.

He'd wanted to see Nabila so badly. He was so lonely. They were finally in the same city, and she was supposed to help make things better, help Matthew get out of this. But their plan seemed impossible at this point, Matthew thought. If he wanted to keep Nabila safe, he had to kill people.

The idea terrified him now. He thought about the logistics of it for a minute, and wondered if he could really do it. Matthew imagined himself walking into a crowd of people with the backpack, then unzipping the side of it, pulling the rifle out and waving it around. People would scream. Then he'd have to shoot them.

He realized, then, that someone would probably shoot him back. He'd known there was the possibility of danger before, but now dying seemed very probable, like he should be ready for it. And then it also seemed clear that the general didn't really care about him. None of the men in the group did. They were throwing him away, pretending like he was doing a good thing, but really it seemed quite horrible.

Was this the kind of thing that AJ had been talking about all along? Was this what he meant when he told them that they'd be powerful? Nothing made sense anymore and Matthew hated everything. His throat was sore and he felt like he was getting a cold. It wouldn't stop raining, and his sleeping bag was completely soaked. He had a plastic sheet for the ground but most of it was keeping his backpack dry so that the rifle would be okay. He'd tried to move it earlier but the bodyguard wouldn't let him.

Eventually Matthew lay back down on his sleeping bag and took a couple of pills. There was nothing else to do.

He heard the sound of a bird, the punctuation of raindrops on the plastic above him. He breathed out a cloud of foggy breath and watched it dissipate. His head started to float. He wished he wasn't alone.

They'd made a fire earlier in the day when it had stopped raining for a bit, but it was too wet now. Matthew and his bodyguard had sat warming their hands, and that's when Matthew found out that it was going to be tonight. His bodyguard had shown him a map, had told him where to go to reach the most targets. That was the word he used. It made Matthew's stomach hurt.

Matthew lay there and realized he hadn't eaten for hours but he wasn't hungry. It seemed unimportant now anyway.

He wanted to talk to Nabila. Matthew tried to picture her face, the way her eyes changed when she smiled, the way her earrings shook when she moved her head. He wondered if her hair had grown longer. He wondered if she was wearing a necklace.

Even with the pills his head was hurting. He wrapped his arms around himself, tried to block out the sound of the rain. He hoped the tarp would hold. He fell asleep and dreamed of drowned woods, of fish swimming past tree trunks.

It's a windy afternoon, the air whipping around the buildings and overtop of roofs. The trees in the garden sway. Waves churn up any water that isn't frozen down in the streets, crashing it up onto ice and concrete walls.

Nabila stirs mud and snowflakes and doesn't say what she knows about Matthew's family. Matthew sits on his hands, watching her, a bubble of mucus appearing and then disappearing up his nostril when he inhales. His hat is too small for his head and makes his ears stick out.

Nabila wants to tell him that she knows he is a liar, but she doesn't want to have to think about his father, with his fists like baseball gloves, with his habit of not treating people like people. So instead she stirs and thinks about how she saw that waves can freeze in shapes in a documentary she'd seen about the Arctic. She thinks about the sun making them into crystals. Ahead of her, Matthew is quiet, his eyes glassy with cold.

"You know," she says, "when the earth gets hotter, we won't have as much snow here. Or maybe no snow at all."

"Really?"

"It'll just be really hot all the time."

"Right. Because of the cars." Matthew looks down at the patch of exposed dirt under the rose bush, his mouth slightly open.

"The earth might just keep getting hotter and hotter," she says. "It might get too hot for us to live. We'd shrivel up in the sun."

He looks up at her, his eyes wide. His chin trembles.

"Maybe then we'll go back to the ocean. Become water people."

"What?"

"Animals came from the water. That's where they were first. So maybe we'll have to go back."

"You mean we'll have to live underwater?"

"No. It would take a long time for that. But maybe we'd live in the shallows, you know, so we could breathe but just always be cooler in the water."

Matthew looks down at the ground, then up at the sun, squinting. "That would be weird," he says.

"Only 'cause we're not used to it." Nabila wipes a couple of snowflakes off her cheek. "Like how we're not really used to the ocean taking over the city, but we're learning. Oceans move and we have to adapt. A long time ago the ocean went through the prairies, stretching all the way from the Arctic to Mexico, cutting North America in two. The ocean is always moving."

Matthew watches her and she can tell he wants to laugh.

"I'm not joking. There really was a sea on the prairies. Water just always finds the easiest way to flow."

"But then why did that water disappear?"

"It didn't disappear, Matthew." Nabila blows hair out of her eyes. "It just moved somewhere else."

"Oh. Right," Matthew says. He finds a stick for himself and begins pushing his food around.

He must know, Nabila thinks. He must lie about his father because he doesn't want people to know the truth. He is scared of people knowing.

She sticks her tongue out and catches a snowflake on the tip. The sun is starting to set already, the sky is getting dark. Wind clears the bushes of snow and tosses a dusting over their heads. Soon, Nabila knows, they'll be able to see the lights of other buildings. She sits back in the snow, closes her eyes for a moment. Vibrations come up from the dirt, the hum of the building's elevators, or the singing of whales in the streets below.

"Do you think people live in this water?" Matthew asks.

"Where?"

"Like below us. When the ocean floods the streets. Is that where people live?"

Nabila opens her eyes. "That's too deep."

"Oh."

"If people live in the water, they'll have to live in the shallow part. You know, so there's rocks and things they can sit on if they get tired. We just need the water to cool off."

"Right."

"And we'll need shade. So water by trees, I guess. The edge of a forest. That would be best."

Matthew nods along and another drip of mucus peeks out his nostril. Nabila looks away. She wipes her own nose with the back of her mitten, wondering if he will catch on. He just keeps watching her.

"Not everyone will survive, you know."

"What?"

"When the water takes over. When cities get destroyed. A lot of people will die."

The drip of mucus reaches the top of Matthew's lip. He still doesn't notice.

"Are we lonely?" he asks.

Nabila thinks about that for a minute. The snow muffles the traffic, and things seem quiet. They'll have to be strong if they are going to survive on top of the building, she thinks. They won't have time to miss people.

"I don't think so," she says.

"Because we have each other."

"Sure."

Matthew smiles. He licks his lip. His jacket isn't done all the way up and his neck is turning red.

Tara Lynn calls to them from the other side of the bushes, and Nabila stands up, and Matthew follows. The sun has gone down and the sky now looks dark blue. Over the edge of the roof wall, Nabila can see thousands of white lights. There are glowing windows and fireflies and maybe the bioluminescence of fish without eyes. She is going to tell Matthew to come look, but when she turns around, he is no longer paying attention.

Nabila woke up throughout the night, snippets of dreams swirling around in her head, places that should have been familiar but that she didn't know. The rain pounded against the window and the tree branches scraped the roof. There was lots of wind, its howling persistent as it rushed down the corridor of the street beyond her room. Headlights came through the gap at the edge of the blinds.

Tierney had texted her later in the night, offered to come home with her, but by then Nabila had already been in bed. Nabila told her that Matthew didn't show, and she hadn't felt like being out with people after that. She needed some time to think.

Tierney said that she was going back to her DJ's place, and that she'd call Nabila in the morning.

It was still so dark by eight a.m. that Nabila wondered if her clock was wrong. She got up and made coffee in the small kitchen, sat at the table and drank it slowly. The rain had stopped but it was still windy, the sky still overcast. The building was settling and creaking.

There was something running around inside of Nabila, an anxiety that she hadn't felt since she was a kid. She used to sit with her mother while she watched reports on the state of the coral reefs, where there would be kilometres of dead coral looking like shrivelled brains, and the feeling would be there. There were other reports, too, ones that would talk about the warming Arctic and radiation, oil spills, tiny plastic particles that were filling the ocean. They explained how an island made up of nothing but garbage was moving across the Pacific, how the seabeds around cities were covered in old car parts and broken refrigerators that were tossed there because it was a cheap place to hide them. Nabila remembered staring at the screen back then, the same feeling of urgency and helplessness that was now pulsing within her. It was knowing that something was wrong, but not knowing what to do to change it.

She just didn't understand. Nabila assumed they would meet when Matthew arrived, but she'd read into things incorrectly, or he'd changed his mind. She didn't know which.

There were day-old baked goods in the fridge and Nabila ate an apple fritter and drank a glass of juice. She turned on the radio and let a German talk show play in the background. She sat there trying to figure things out.

The more Nabila thought about it, the more enraged she became. This was not what she'd signed up for. She was doing him a favour and working to right her wrong, but he didn't get to push her away and pull her back on a whim, didn't get to ignore her completely.

That wasn't the Matthew that she knew, though, and something didn't quite sit right. He'd seemed so terrified when he'd asked her for help to escape. He'd been lonely and anxious and now suddenly he wasn't responding. He hadn't texted her for days, so she'd assumed he didn't have his cellphone with him, but then suddenly he sent her that note and photo.

Nabila wanted some answers. She'd flown all the way to Berlin, and she needed to know what was going on. Maybe Matthew was just being frustrating, but maybe he was in danger.

So Nabila decided that she was going to try and find him. She needed to hear from him, and if he was in Berlin like his text had said he was, she was going to investigate. At least then she would be able to understand what was happening.

She messaged Tierney, but when she didn't respond after a few minutes, she called her. It rang a few times, was cut off, and Nabila dialled her number again. This time Tierney answered. Her voice was groggy. Nabila told her that she needed her help, and that she wanted to find out what was going on.

"What do you have in mind?" Tierney asked, and Nabila told her how she was thinking of just going to that squatters' corner place this morning, trying to see if they could find him. She could hear Tierney slowly waking up as she talked. Nabila heard her move around, heard a door opening and closing. She said that if Matthew really was there, like he said he was, she wanted to hear from him directly.

"I like it," Tierney said, then laughed, said it sounded like one of her own plans.

That caused Nabila to worry a bit. She asked how rough that part of the woods really was. Tierney said she'd been there a few times, because she once had a friend who was living there. They shouldn't go at night. During the day might be okay, though. It would be even better if they had a guy with them.

"Hey, give me a minute," Tierney said, and then Nabila could hear her having a conversation, heard the lower sounds of a man's voice.

She waited.

"He's in!" Tierney reported a moment later. "Ricardo. My DJ. He's up for any adventure that includes me."

Tierney giggled, and then Nabila could hear her moving again, wondered if the DJ was still there, holding Tierney around her waist, nuzzling her shoulders. Nabila wasn't sure she wanted to turn this thing into a group expedition, but if Tierney was concerned about safety, then bringing him was probably a good idea.

"Can we go now?" she asked.

"Now? Like, right now?"

"Or soon?"

"Maybe give us half an hour," Tierney said, and then she was giggling again, and Nabila heard more moving and shuffling. She said that was fine, but Tierney didn't respond. Nabila hung up the phone.

Now that the plan was set, she started to second-guess it. But she needed to talk to Matthew, and this was the only way she could think of to make that happen. She hoped he was still there. And she felt better knowing that Tierney was bringing Ricardo. She would rather not have to go through anything similar to last night.

Tierney and Ricardo were waiting for her at the train station. It was the same stop that she knew from the night before, close to the club with the train, and also, apparently, in the vicinity of Ricardo's apartment. Tierney gave her a hug and Ricardo introduced himself by kissing her on both cheeks. She hadn't paid much attention to him the night before, and now took in his green eyes and wide shoulders, a tattoo on his forearm of an open book. She couldn't tell if he had styled his hair with gel or if it was just greasy.

They led Nabila down a couple of main streets before they turned onto a smaller road with cheap restaurants and an Oxfam on the corner. Tierney talked nonstop. She told Nabila how she'd waited until Ricardo had finished his last set, and then the two of them had gone to his apartment building where there was a courtyard with patio chairs. They'd listened to the rain fall all around them, and it was like they were in a movie, Tierney said, where it was like every little detail had been set into place. She put her arm around Ricardo's waist as she said it, and he kissed her neck. Nabila turned her attention away.

They turned down another seedy street, then crossed a rundown park where the forest started. Tierney said that she'd filled Ricardo in, that they were both operating on the understanding that Matthew was being a jackass, and that they would both back her up with whatever she decided to do.

Nabila had found the directions again beforehand, and had also learned that this part of the forest was an unmonitored stretch where people passing through stayed for a few days or even a few months. It was actually a relatively small patch of land, but the forest could be pretty thick.

She had her purse slung across her shoulder, and in a compartment inside it, Matthew's passport. She wondered if he'd really be here. Part of her wasn't expecting to find him.

"So, you've got to give us some details," Tierney said as they started down a narrow path cut between the trees. "What's your Matthew look like? Tall, short? Well-built? Who are we looking for?"

Nabila tried to describe him, but she found it difficult. Pale, was the only concrete thing that she came up with. Tierney found that hilarious.

When the forest started to get thicker, Ricardo offered to take the lead. "It's a good idea," Tierney said. "You never know who's going to jump out."

Nabila was starting to question things again. She wasn't sure if this had been the best way to approach the situation with Matthew, but she tried to remind herself that she didn't have a lot of options, and this was a way that could get her some answers. She needed to do this.

The air was cold and it felt like it might rain again. It was the early afternoon by now, but still so overcast that it seemed either much earlier or much later. Ricardo led the way, then Tierney, and Nabila followed behind. It was like being back in the Fairytale Forest, she thought, waiting for something to emerge from the undergrowth. Once again, she didn't really have a clear idea of what she was walking into.

There were no sounds of cars now, nothing but the wind above them and the crunch of dead leaves beneath their feet. Some trees still had their branches full, their leaves yellow or dried and waving, but many of them were almost completely bare. They could see through the forest on both sides, just trunks and branches, the odd splash of green or a grey rock.

And then Nabila could see something orange. It was always easy to spot things that didn't belong in nature, because nature never had lines that were too straight, or colours that were too different. This orange was in the shape of a perfect triangle, and a moment later, Nabila realized it was a tent. There was a small clearing and she saw a bucket, a firepit with a circle of small stones. "Alright, now we're talking," she heard Ricardo say. "We'll try to find someone we can ask about him."

There was no one by the orange tent, so they kept on moving. They passed a grey tarp with a man lying beneath it, snoring, and then another tent that looked like it had knife slashes along the side. The fabric was flapping in the breeze.

They stepped over a small stream and then saw someone kneeling by the water. He stood and looked at them, and Nabila could see that he'd just finished brushing his teeth. "Hallo," Ricardo called over, then kept speaking German. The man spoke back in a quiet voice. Then there was some gesturing and pointing.

"Aren't you glad we brought him?" Tierney said, nudging Nabila. She nodded.

From somewhere in the treetops, a crow called, and Nabila jumped a bit. She hoped Tierney hadn't noticed.

The man talking to Ricardo looked over at them, and then stuck his toothbrush behind his ear as if it were a pen. Nabila tried to figure out what he was saying, but all she could catch was his tone—mildly interested, receptive to Ricardo's questions. She caught herself holding her breath.

Then Ricardo turned toward her and Tierney, gestured for them to come forward. "This is Max," he said, and they stepped closer and smiled, and Max smiled, too. He was missing a couple of teeth. "Max thinks he maybe saw Matthew yesterday. Or at least there's a young guy farther downriver who doesn't speak any German who just arrived. He's got a blue tarp, wears a backpack. Sound about right?"

They all looked at Nabila, and she shrugged. "Could be."

Ricardo turned back to Max, and they talked for another moment. Then he clapped Max on the back and the man turned to wave at them, then disappeared into the woods.

"See?" Ricardo said, moving toward them. "Not everyone here is all that bad."

Tierney grabbed his hand, gave him a quick peck on the cheek. "Which way did he say? That way? I wanna find this Matthew."

She took off along the edge of the stream, pulling Ricardo along behind her. Nabila ran a bit to catch up. They didn't go far before they came upon a grouping of tents in a larger clearing: there were a couple of grey ones, a few loose sleeping bags drying out on tree stumps, and then off toward the side, a blue tarp. Ricardo and Tierney were already making their way toward it. They all stopped at the edge of the tarp where it was tied to a tree.

"There's nobody here," Tierney said.

Nabila found that she was both disappointed and relieved.

The tarp was secured to the ground on the other side so that the space beneath it was small and sloping. There was a sleeping bag and a folded blanket on the ground, both sodden, and a couple of empty granola bar wrappers. They walked around the tarp a couple of times, tried to see if there was anything else of interest, but it was just dirt and sticks.

"So," Ricardo said. "What now?"

And then something moved in the woods behind him, and Nabila realized they were being watched. Tierney noticed it too, and Ricardo must have seen them staring, because he swivelled around, stood up very straight.

He was partially hidden behind a couple of tree trunks, but Nabila recognized the colour of his hair, the slope of his shoulders. It was strange to see him after so long. She stared at him, took a deep breath.

"Matthew?"

He came out from between the trees, his eyes flitting back and forth from the ground to Nabila's face.

Nabila stepped forward. Matthew's eyes were wide. He looked like a deer, Nabila thought. Ready at any moment to spring for cover. This was the Matthew she'd always known, and she felt herself relax a bit. Their last few exchanges had made her worry he'd changed.

"What are you doing here?" He whispered.

He was wearing a backpack, just like Max had said. He must be constantly carrying everything he owned around with him, she realized. A tarp didn't provide that much security.

"I brought what you asked for. And I want to talk to you. I wanted to talk to you last night, but you didn't show."

Matthew dropped his eyes. "I'm sorry about that."

"What the hell, Matthew?"

"I'm sorry Nabila. But you should go. I'm not alone here."

"What does that mean?"

"Someone's staying with me, watching me."

"From the group? Shit. I thought maybe they caught you. Look, just come with us. Right now."

"I can't."

"Why not?"

"Just don't come to the market by the station here tonight. Just stay away. Okay?"

"What's going on, Matthew?"

"Please, Nabila. Just stay away."

He looked tired, she thought. Really tired. Not just that he hadn't slept, but rather like he'd forgotten sleep was important. His eyes were glassy and red, and his face had lost some of its shape, all of the edges now softened. He had a bit of a beard, maybe a week's worth of growth, and she wasn't used to that. For a moment he looked like he was going to say something else, but instead he sneezed.

"Hey man," Ricardo said, stepping back up again. "I don't know what's going on here, but you better talk to her."

"Ricardo, it's okay."

"No, it's not okay." He turned back to Matthew. "What's wrong with you? You high?"

"Ricardo, just let me talk to him."

Matthew was staring at Ricardo, his mouth slightly open. He shifted his feet as if contemplating running away.

"Look, just come with us now," Nabila said. "I've got what you need to get home. We'll get away from them and make a run for it."

"Hey," a voice suddenly said from behind them. Nabila spun around, Ricardo and Tierney doing the same, and found a large man in a dark jacket standing beside Matthew's tarp. Nabila froze. She recognized him from the night before, when he'd come up to her in the club, asked to buy her a drink. She forced herself to stand tall, to root her feet into the ground.

"Hey," he said again. "Get out."

Ricardo almost laughed. "What is this? You his bodyguard?"

"Yeah. And I said get out."

Nabila looked back at Matthew, who was watching everything unfold without saying anything. Now she saw that he didn't have a choice.

Matthew looked at her. "I'm sorry, Nabila."

His eyes had gotten really red, and she remembered the way he'd looked sitting in her laboratory, trying to get her to want him to stay.

He hadn't really changed, at least not in the way she'd worried about. If anything, he looked confused. Drowsy.

"You're going to make me remove you in a second," the man said, and Nabila turned back to find him staring right at her.

"Don't hurt her," Matthew said quietly.

"She should leave if she doesn't want to get hurt."

"Alright, cool it," Ricardo said. He gestured for Tierney and Nabila to lead the way around the other side of the tarp, and Tierney started walking, but Nabila didn't know what to do. She didn't want to leave Matthew.

Then Ricardo turned around and swung his fist and hit Matthew's face. Matthew fell backwards into a tree, and then the other man was lunging at Ricardo with both his fists in the air and his eyes wide. Ricardo was quick, though: he ducked two punches, then hit the man in the back of the head. Then he had his hand on Nabila's elbow, was pulling her away from them.

"Come on," he yelled at her, and Nabila still didn't want to leave Matthew, but his bodyguard was looking right at her, ready to get off the ground and lunge. So she ran.

They followed Tierney back the way they'd come, past the tents, along the stream. They were moving so fast that Nabila couldn't tell where they were going, but Ricardo and Tierney seemed to know, had no hesitation. The three of them ran through the forest, dodging trees.

He watched them leave, heard the sound of their footsteps long after they disappeared from view. He tried to stop his shaking. The back of his head was throbbing, and his jaw felt like it had shifted sideways. He was seeing spots of black and white. His bodyguard was getting up from the ground, cradling his neck.

He loved Nabila and hated Nabila, and sometimes the emotions would come in quick succession, especially when he wasn't prepared for things. She'd suddenly just been there, standing right in front of him. He'd barely been able to figure out words.

A few people had come out of their tents, were looking over to see what had caused the commotion, but soon the forest grew quiet again. His bodyguard went back to his tarp behind a clump of trees and then Matthew retreated beneath his tarp, too, settled on the ground. He'd looked for a place that was dry but everything was still wet.

His fingers were stiff from cold, and the muscles in his injured leg now hurt all the time. He didn't need a bandage anymore, but the scab was thick and itchy.

He figured he should eat something. He had a couple more granola bars left, but the thought of unwrapping one made him feel sick. It would be too sweet. He wasn't that hungry, anyway. He could last another few hours.

Nabila had been here and now she was gone, and Matthew thought about how worried she'd looked, how her eyes had been so concerned. He'd remembered what she looked like, but somehow it had been different seeing her for real again, seeing how she talked and crossed her arms in front of her body. Those kinds of things were sometimes easier to forget.

Now he still had to do the mission because the bodyguard knew who she was and would go find her. Matthew couldn't escape and couldn't make sure she was safe. It had all become a mess and now it was only a few more hours away. Matthew wasn't ready.

For a while he tried to sort out the way he felt about Nabila, what she would think about everything, but the process was taking too much energy. He wondered how his mother and sisters would find out. He pictured his mother sitting at the kitchen table, her face in her hands, unsure of how he turned out this way. Matthew wasn't sure himself. There were too many things to feel, and it was hurting him. He took another pill. Better to not feel at this stage.

He got up and stood just outside of the tarp, saw how a tiny bit of sunshine was breaking through the clouds and was then swallowed back up.

He would leave the tarp up, he decided, strung between the trees that would get covered in snow. It would hang there all winter, and maybe squirrels would come by, or deer, or a drifter who'd sit drinking in the dryness. The thought of that made him feel a bit better. He walked over to the stream, dipped his fingers in the icy water and washed his face.

His nose was stuffed, and he felt like he might be getting a fever. His jaw felt strange from the punch and he was sure the place where his head had hit the tree was raised and his scalp pink. He crawled back beneath the tarp, tried to get warm. He just wished for it all to be over.

The snow is melting, and there are blossoms in the flower bed, tiny green buds that smell like rain. In the streets below, ice breaks apart and floats away. Narwhals come up to breathe.

Matthew is attentive today. Whenever Nabila says something he follows along, digging and stirring and collecting sticks. It's warm enough now to take off their mittens. The ground is still a bit frozen, but they can chip away at the soil, bring up little pieces of dirt to mix into their stew. They also have bits of old cedar, a couple of decomposing flower petals from the season before.

There won't be a lot of ice in the streets with the earth warming, Nabila knows, but there'll probably still be some. A thin layer, too thin for polar bears. Beneath it the water will be clear, because it is always clearest when it's cold, and there'll be cars at the bottom like old shipwrecks. Mussels and sea urchins will clamp onto their roofs.

When she describes those things, Matthew can't imagine them. "I don't know what cars look like underwater," he says.

"Just try to think of it."

He closes his eyes, screws up his face to concentrate.

She decides to try explaining the stars they'll see instead. She talks about the constellations and how they'll still be the same as the ones in the sky now. Matthew listens and covers his left hand with dirt.

"There's a line that you have to look for, three stars in a row," she says. She draws them with a stick. "See?"

Matthew glances over and nods.

"Then there's four stars, and they make a kind of cup. That's the dipper part. That's how you know you found it."

Matthew looks at her drawings in the earth and frowns. "Are they behind the ozone?"

"What?"

"The ozone that you were talking about. Before. The one that was disappearing and making the ocean flood the city."

Nabila stares at him. "They're in outer space."

"Oh."

"The ozone is like a shield. For the earth." She blows a puff of air out her mouth. "When it disappears the sun will come straight in. It's disappearing because there's too much pollution in the air."

"Oh."

Matthew stares at his hand again, covering the base of his wrist with dirt. Nabila stands up and drops her stick.

"And the flooding is because the air around us is getting warmer," she says. "Remember how I already told you that?" She walks over to the wall and back again, then makes a circle around Matthew. She breaks a twig off the nearest hedge and folds it into smaller and smaller pieces. "All the ice in the Arctic will melt and that makes the oceans rise into the city." She drops the twig.

"Right."

She frowns. "I feel like you should remember this."

"I did remember it."

"No you didn't."

Matthew watches her, his hand still buried. She stands in front of him.

She is getting tired of Matthew's pretending. He never pretends properly in the game, can't really see all the things she wants to imagine, but when it comes to other things he sometimes makes stuff up. She knows that he doesn't really understand why the world is heating up. She'll have to explain it again.

"If the streets are already flooded, there's a big problem with our air. Parts of it are like poison. It's all because of the cars and trucks, and the garbage, and all the factories pumping out pollution."

"I don't want there to be poison air."

"Nobody wants there to be poison air."

"But then what do we do? If we breathe it in? Will we die?"

Nabila thinks about the question. Matthew watches her, his eyes big and round, and she realizes she likes being able to figure out the answers. To make things in their game work. She thinks about how you could get rid of poison. The only way would be to get the air out of the person's lungs.

"We don't have to die," she says. "We just have to get the poison out."

"How?"

"I'll show you."

She makes Matthew unbury his hand and lie on the hard dirt on his back. Then she makes him close his eyes. Beyond the hedge, she can hear Samir and Tara Lynn reading a book. She walks over to Matthew and then kneels beside him.

"I came back from somewhere and found you like this," she says quietly, "lying poisoned on the ground. But I'll help you get fresh air."

Matthew is very still. He keeps his eyes squeezed shut, and Nabila leans over him and looks at the freckles between his eyes, at the holes of his nostrils. She needs to blow into his mouth because mouth-to-mouth is how you save someone's life, but she also knows that it is like kissing, which people like to do, which her parents sometimes do with their faces pressed together and their hands wrapped around each other's bodies.

She bends over, slowly, and puts her mouth against Matthew's. His lips are warmer than she thinks they'll be. She blows out a puff of air. Then she opens her eyes, and so does he, and she pulls her mouth away, and his eyes are still wide and unblinking and staring at her.

She sits back, and he sits up, and then they don't look at each other. Nabila plays with the belt loop on her jeans.

Finally she says, "When I blew clean air into your mouth, it took up all the space in your lungs. So then you breathed the poison out." She swallows. She looks over and Matthew nods, his hands held in his lap. His cheeks are red.

"Okay," Matthew says.

Her face is hot, and she hopes she isn't blushing like he is. She picks at her nail. She shifts her feet and sits cross-legged.

"Maybe," Matthew says slowly, and then stops. She looks at him and he looks at the ground. "Maybe next time, you're the one who breathes in poison, and I can save you."

"Okay," Nabila says. She picks a rose petal off the dirt. "You mean, like right now?"

"Okay."

Matthew gets up and Nabila takes his place on the ground. She lies on her back and crosses her arms over her chest, and then feels silly, so she lays them down at her sides. She can suddenly hear the traffic of the city, the driving and honking that shouldn't have been there.

Beneath her, the earth is cool. She hears a bird chirp, and then the sunlight on her face is blocked by a shadow hovering over her.

It is different being the one lying down. She doesn't know what's happening until his lips are right there, pressing against hers. He blows a puff of air at her and she lets it into her mouth. Her heart is in her ears and his mouth is still there, and she opens her eyes and can't see anything except for the tiny hairs of his eyebrow.

He pulls away and she sits up. She can hear his breathing. The street noises are loud again, and she thinks about how she needs to forget about the cars, to go back to the water and all the ocean creatures.

"Was that okay?" Matthew whispers.

She glances at him then. He is flushed, staring at her, his hands on the ground grabbing pieces of dirt. His lips look wet. She runs the back of her hand over her own mouth.

"Now I'm clear of poison," she says.

Matthew nods.

She stands up, and he does too, still holding dirt in his hands. He drops it when he notices her frowning at his clasped fingers, and it falls to the ground and lands near his shoes. He rubs his hands together to brush off the rest.

Tara Lynn calls them then, saying that Matthew's sisters are downstairs, and Nabila comes out from behind the hedge and walks toward the gazebo. She knows Matthew will follow her. She feels a bit light but also solid, like her legs are ready to run or jump or kick into the air. Like she'll be able to survive when most other people burn up.

As they were running, it had started to rain again. Nabila was kicking up mud and old leaves, trying to follow in the places where Ricardo or Tierney had stepped. There were exposed roots and tree trunks that they had to jump over. There were branches flung backwards that hit her in the shoulder.

She thought that maybe she should have just grabbed his arm and made him run with them, that maybe he could have gotten away. She was glad she hadn't given him the passport because his bodyguard would have probably taken it. But now she didn't know what to do.

They exited the thick part of the woods and ended up back on the narrow path, then made it out to the park and stopped on the grass to catch their breath. Nabila wondered if the bodyguard would suddenly emerge from between the trees, start barrelling toward them. They were exposed out in the middle of the field.

But he didn't appear, and they were left with just one another. The rain started to get heavier.

In nature, Nabila knew, everything took the easiest path. Nothing did anything that was unnecessary, that wasn't efficient. Sometimes she wished that people behaved that way. She felt like it would help her understand them better.

"Why'd you have to punch him?" she moaned at Ricardo.

He was standing in front of her, pulling the hood from his sweatshirt up over his hair. "He was going to unleash his bodyguard," he said. "That boyfriend of yours, man, I don't know. What's his problem?"

Nabila sighed. The rain was making the air foggy.

"He's not your boyfriend, is he?"

Nabila turned to look at Tierney, who was standing with her arms crossed, her eyes narrowed.

"I mean, that's what you said. But it's not true."

Nabila met Tierney's eyes, and then looked down at the ground. On her other side, Ricardo was bouncing on his heels and there was the squelch of wet grass beneath his running shoes. He looked from Tierney to Nabila.

"Wait, what?" he said. Then he shook his head. "Doesn't matter. They were threatening us."

"Matthew wasn't," Nabila said quietly, her eyes not leaving the ground. "He would have come with us if he wasn't so scared. Couldn't you see he was scared?"

Nabila had been unsure about Matthew this morning, because all she'd had to understand him were his messages, the fact that he hadn't shown up last night. But now that she'd seen him, had spoken to him in person, she knew that hadn't been Matthew. He was in trouble. She put her hand over her purse, felt for the edge of his passport through the fabric. She should make sure it didn't get wet.

"He was trying to get away from these people, but looks like they found him," she said. "Or he never got away in the first place, I don't know."

Ricardo shook his head. "I'm so confused."

"Did you hear what he told me?" Nabila said. "About not going to the market tonight? I don't know why he said that."

Tierney looked at Ricardo, then looked at Nabila. "It sounds like he doesn't want to see you," she said.

Nabila rubbed her forehead. There was rain running off the tip of her nose now, and she realized that they should find a place inside.

"Hey," Ricardo said.

Nabila glanced up and saw that he was trying to hail a cab that was passing on the street.

"We're not going back, right? It's enough for now." He took a few steps toward the road as the car started to slow down.

They ended up at Ricardo's apartment. Somehow Nabila had gotten stuck sitting in the middle of the back seat, and found that she had to sit back because Tierney kept trying to look at Ricardo when he talked. Their clothes were soaked. The cab sprayed a wall of water up onto the sidewalk as they rounded corners, and Nabila thought about Matthew's blue tarp, about the forest floor beneath it that was slowly being reclaimed.

The apartment was on the fourth floor, a large open space with a small kitchen and bathroom, where everything seemed to be in black or wood tones. Ricardo gave them large t-shirts to change into; Tierney's had tour dates for a band called Silbermond, and Nabila's was a group called Unheilig. Even though the shirt was long, she left her pants on. Tierney took hers off.

Nabila put water on to boil for tea and stood waiting in the kitchen. Ricardo and Tierney were standing by the open window in the living room, sharing a cigarette and blowing smoke out into the rain, talking to each other in low voices. Nabila thought at first that they were discussing her, that they were trying to figure out what was going on with her and Matthew, but then she realized that they didn't really care. Tierney had her hand on his hip and he kept pushing a stray strand of hair behind her ear. They were probably waiting for her to leave.

Nabila was tired, though, and she wanted some caffeine. She stood there waiting for the kettle to steam and thought about heat waves that boiled clams in tidepools, how they were stuck in place with no chance of a way out.

She made tea and brought mugs for the three of them into the living room. Tierney left Ricardo at the window and came to sit next to her on the couch.

"I think his bodyguard's got his phone," Nabila said. "I actually saw him at the club last night."

"What the hell, Nabila? I think you need to leave Matthew alone," Tierney said. "I mean, I know you came here to see him, but this all seems messed up."

Nabila took the teabag out of her mug, left it on a napkin on the table. The liquid from the sachet started to bleed across the paper.

"He's in with a rough crowd." Nabila took a sip of her tea and the heat shocked the roof of her mouth.

"And you're worried about him."

She nodded. "He needs my help."

"What if you just called the police and told them Matthew's being held against his will? Maybe they can help him. That bodyguard will probably kill us if we go back, but they might do something."

"I just, I don't know about that," Nabila said. She took another sip. "I don't think he's done anything wrong, but I don't know what he's been up to. And what if there's more of them? I don't want to make things dangerous for Matthew."

"That's why I think you should just leave him alone. It's not like he's your brother or anything," Tierney said.

Nabila stared into her teacup.

"Matthew won't hurt me," she said. "His bodyguard might, but Matthew won't. I know he won't."

Tierney sighed, then got up and walked back over to the window. Ricardo slid his hand up the edge of her shirt and pulled her toward him. Nabila took another sip of tea.

She didn't think she could go back to the woods. The only other place she had was the market he'd mentioned. She wasn't sure why he said that, if he was trying to be cryptic and really did think he could meet her there, or if something was going to happen at that place. He could have been trying to warn her about something. The thought sent a shiver down her back. But she had his passport, and she needed to try to get it to him so at least he had a chance if he escaped. Maybe she could still somehow help him sneak away.

Tierney was giggling by the window, and the rain had started coming down hard again. Nabila drank more tea and felt warmer. She owed it to Matthew to not just leave him. And going to the market seemed like the only option she had.

S pring is almost over, and Nabila loves the rooftop garden when everything is blooming. There are roses and asters, purple clematis that snake up the side walls. The small trees are full of leaves, and their spot behind the hedges smells of wet earth and worms.

Nabila tries to explain that the water level is rising because more of the ice is melting. A huge part of the Arctic is gone now, she tells Matthew, which is why the streets are flooded up to the fourth or fifth floor of their building. It will continue to rise, higher and higher, because there is so much carbon dioxide and the world just keeps getting warmer. Things are being destroyed.

Matthew sits on the dirt and listens to her with his mouth hanging open. She tells him they have to do something. He asks what.

"Have an escape plan," Nabila says. "So we don't get trapped."

"Okay," he says.

"Any ideas?"

"No." He plays with the leaves of the bush beside him. "Well, maybe we can find the pirate ship," he says. "Maybe they'll let us on."

"They're pirates, Matthew." Nabila shakes her head. "They won't just let us on. But maybe we can stow away."

"Stow away?"

"You know, like hide on the ship without them seeing us. In the hold. Or in an apple barrel."

"Okay. Sure."

Nabila goes to the wall and holds up her imaginary telescope. "There's lots of whales today. And the giant octopus. But I don't see the ship yet." She comes back over to Matthew and sits in the dirt next to him. She breaks off a stick and pulls up some grass and starts mixing things together in the dirt. "We'll need food," she says. "We should make some to take with us."

Matthew starts stirring next to her. He digs a little hole with his hand and fills it in with dried flower petals.

"Maybe the air is poisoned again, too," he says. "Maybe you breathed some in?"

Nabila looks over, and he stares at his flower petals, mixing them with his fingers.

"I don't think so," she says.

"Why not?"

"Because it just isn't."

"Oh."

His fingers are incredibly pink, Nabila notices. They are chubby around the knuckles, and he has dirt under most nails. As she watches him, he sits back and stops stirring. Nabila pretends not to notice. She plucks a few leaves and adds them to her mixture, then reaches out and takes some of Matthew's dried flower petals. It is going to be a curry, she decides, something that will give them energy if they have to travel somewhere else. They'll have to collect some water too, because the floodwater is probably too salty to drink.

"What if I want to stay here?" Matthew says suddenly. His voice is quiet.

"But the pirate ship was your idea."

"I don't like it anymore. I think we should stay. I think the game is good like this. With our forest up here and the water below and the sometimes-poisoned air. We should keep it the same."

Nabila looks at him. "That won't work."

Matthew's bottom lip quivers. Nabila sits back and puffs her cheeks up with breath. He is like a bird, she thinks. A bird with tiny bones, and she could crush them without meaning to. She lets the air out of her mouth slowly.

"Look, let's just make food," she says. She hands him a stick.

Matthew stirs the dirt again without saying anything. Nabila crumbles some of the rose petals into little bits. Samir is saying more words these days, and she can hear him from the gazebo, asking for apple juice. Tara Lynn tells him there is only a little bit left.

"How about we stay here for a year," Matthew says. His head is down and it is like he is talking to the earth.

"A year?"

"Yeah. We stay here for the summer, and the fall, and then another winter and spring. Then we can stow away on the pirate ship."

Nabila frowns. "But you won't really be here in the summer, and in the fall, I don't know if we'll even pick you up anymore."

Matthew looks at her. "Why not?"

"'Cause I'm starting piano lessons next year. And my swimming will be on Tuesdays and Thursdays. Mom says we'll have to go straight from school, and Tara Lynn will bring my bathing suit or piano books or whatever I need when she picks me up."

She plucks another couple of leaves off the bush, and then realizes that Matthew is still staring at her. She looks back at him.

"You won't pick me up anymore?" he whispers.

"I'll still see you at school," she says, even though she knows they never talk at school. She knows Matthew knows that, too. She drops the leaves into her curry. When she glances at him again, she sees that his eyes are red.

"But what will happen to our forest?" he asks. His voice cracks. "I mean, without us here, there won't be a forest. Or the ocean water in the streets below. It will just be a building with plants on top."

"Well, I'll still play up here," Nabila says, and then realizes that was the wrong thing to say. She flicks some dirt back and forth. "I mean, just so it won't disappear."

Matthew holds on to his stirring stick with both hands and bends it back and forth. His whole face is red now, and he wipes his eyes with the back of his sleeve. Nabila notices two wet streaks on the fabric. She sighs.

She thinks about saying sorry, but then she can't exactly figure out what for. Maybe for making him cry, she supposes, but she hadn't meant to. He cries so easily.

She hears a snapping sound, and looks down and sees that Matthew has broken the stick and holds half in each hand. He seems surprised. He drops both pieces on the ground and covers them up with dirt.

"Come on," Nabila says, and taps his shoulder as gently as possible. "Let's go see if we can find the pirate ship."

She gets up, and Matthew does too, but she has a feeling she already knows what they'll find beyond the wall. The ocean water has risen, almost to the height of the rooftop, and soon it will all pour in and drown things.

That morning she'd been so angry with Matthew, but now there was a fear taking hold of Nabila, a fear that she'd left Matthew alone for far too long and this was the result. He'd looked so insignificant standing there in the forest, his wet hair plastered to his scalp.

She'd finished her tea and changed back into her wet clothes, left Tierney and Ricardo standing by the window again. Now that the excitement of finding Matthew was over, they no longer seemed interested in anything she was doing. She wasn't even sure they noticed when she left. Outside, it was no longer raining. She walked to the S-Bahn and rode it back to the part of the city that was familiar.

Even in the rooftop garden, where it had only been the two of them, she always knew they'd survived because of her. That she was the stronger one. She'd saved him because he was there, but she wasn't sure she would have gone out of her way for him. Things had always been like that between them: she'd been at the graduation party, so she'd cleaned up his arm; she'd had free time on her lunch break, so she'd texted him. Sometimes he'd been almost like an afterthought. But she knew now that she was worried about him too, really worried. She wondered how long that feeling had been there.

She walked back toward Café Arboretum and watched the war tree wave in the wind. Tierney had probably been right, she realized. Maybe Matthew was more like a little brother, like the way she thought about Samir. Most of the time he was on her periphery, was sometimes annoying. But then she'd fly halfway around the world to find him.

Back at the café, she walked past the *Closed* sign and through the empty rooms, heard the wooden floors creak beneath her feet. Then she climbed the fire escape to the upper level and almost slipped on the wet stairs.

She had a hot shower and then changed into warmer clothing. Even though the rain had finally stopped, Nabila found that she couldn't quite get comfortable.

She went into the apartment's kitchen and sliced a cucumber. She sat and ate at the small table without turning on the lights. Only the stove light was on, a tiny rectangle of illumination in the corner. She ate without thinking about how it tasted.

She'd looked up the area around Matthew's intersection and found an outdoor market a few streets over. It was the only one in the area, so she figured that's what he'd been talking about. It was right by a bend in the river. There would be lots of people around, Nabila told herself. There would be places to run if she didn't want to stay.

It wasn't that she was afraid of Matthew. She wasn't sure he could ever scare her. But she found that she was wary of whoever was behind him, and if there was something more going on that she didn't understand.

Nabila washed her dishes and left them to dry. She put on her coat and mittens, a green toque that Tierney had said she could wear. Then she realized she'd gotten ready far too early and took everything off and sat back down again. She wanted to get there in the early evening, so she could be there if Matthew was arriving and look out for him. She figured she should wait a bit longer before leaving. Nabila turned on the radio, took out her phone. She got up and cleaned a smattering of crumbs off the counter.

She looked up the location again, checked three times that her phone had enough battery. She assessed the size of her pockets, made sure there were no holes in the bottom for things to fall through. She put her purse across her shoulders and checked to make sure Matthew's passport was still there. Then she pulled it back out, and opened it up to his picture page. He stared up at her with his wide eyes. She closed it back up and put it away.

It was still too early but Nabila was ready to leave. She walked down the stairs and realized she was nervous, tried to calm herself down by taking a few deep breaths and imagining the sway of the war tree above her.

She wondered if Matthew would even be there. She knew she had to be careful, had to watch out for his bodyguard or anyone else that looked suspicious. A car honked on the street next to her on the way to the S-Bahn, and she jumped. Then she was annoyed with herself, forced herself to stay focused.

She got on the train and stood because it was crowded. There were two little boys next to her who were sucking rock candy, and both had red and blue stains across their chins. The floor was slippery with the rain from people's boots.

A lot of people were getting off at Nabila's stop, and she followed the crowds out onto the platform, then up the stairs toward the exit and out to street level.

It was dark now, and the air was cold. The rain had stopped but it had chilled everything. Nabila pulled the toque over her ears and felt the world muffle. There were strings of lights across an awning ahead of her, flashes of green and gold and red, and the murmur of lots of people talking. The crowd was heading to the market to the right. It was glowing in the night, shimmering, and she imagined that it was a world underwater. She squinted her eyes and it was easier to see.

The crowd was bottlenecking at the entranceway. Nabila broke away from the group and walked over to the edge of the road, stared down one way and then another. She walked the length of the block, then back again, then stood around for a while pretending to talk on her phone. Her fingers were cold. People were wearing hats or had hoods pulled up onto their foreheads, but she tried to look at their faces anyway, tried to connect with their eyes.

She didn't recognize anyone.

There was a small ache in Nabila's stomach. Something didn't feel right, and she swallowed it back down, but it took shape again in the back of her throat. She should leave, she thought. She took a deep breath, held it in her mouth. She should walk away right now, get back on the subway. She should spend the evening sitting in Tierney's apartment.

But then she saw him. Matthew was crossing the street, looking down the road toward her, though not at her. She stood up straight.

He had a dark coat on, a dark hat. He was wearing his backpack. Nabila's first thought was that he looked cold. His hands were in his pockets, and his shoulders were hunched over, curved inward. He moved slowly and his gaze was focused down on the ground ahead. He looked small, she thought. He walked as if he were still a little boy.

Nabila stood where she was. Matthew stepped up onto the curb and started moving down the sidewalk toward her. There were lots of people around, heading toward and away from the market, but he dodged them all. He was alone, she realized, and she couldn't see his bodyguard anywhere. He could be watching them from a distance, she supposed. She surveyed the crowd again but still didn't see him.

Matthew kept walking toward her. He was favouring one side, she realized, limping. He was coming up to her, just a few feet away now. Nabila stared at him. It was as if he could feel it. He stopped, turned his head, looked up. He found her eyes.

They didn't move for a moment. The air was cold, and they could see each other's breath. People walked past them in hats and mittens, carrying shopping bags and paper cups of coffee or hot apple cider, but the two of them stayed still. Someone brushed against Nabila's arm. A few feet away a kid slipped and fell on the ground, then picked herself back up.

Nabila hadn't really gotten a good look at Matthew in the forest. Now he was standing beneath a streetlight, and she could see the age lines on his forehead, a cut that was starting to scab on his cheek. He had ragged blonde stubble across the bottom half of his face, and there was rain or sweat caught in it. His barely there eyelashes were blinking fast.

He was watching her, too.

Nabila noticed as he dropped his gaze, focused on her scarf, her mouth. Then he turned toward the ground.

"You aren't supposed to be here," he said, still looking at the cobblestones. She almost couldn't hear him through the noise of passing people.

"Why not?" Nabila shifted her feet. She glanced around. "I thought you wanted to get away."

He looked up at her, his eyes so blue they were almost silver. He kept blinking. "I told you not to come here tonight."

A chill went down Nabila's body. She stared at him, and the ache was back in her stomach.

"Matthew, what's happening?"

He didn't say anything.

"Matthew, is everything okay?"

He looked down, shrugged his shoulders. People kept walking by.

Something wasn't right. Nabila realized she was holding her breath again. The streetlights were changing, a bus was coming down the road. Someone was singing a song in German. The sidewalk was slippery, and Matthew was taking a hand out of his pocket so that he could wipe his nose with a Kleenex.

"I couldn't escape," Matthew said. "They had another plan for me."

Nabila stared at him.

"But you weren't supposed to be here. Why are you here, Nabila?"

He whined the last part, like a grumpy child, and she was suddenly very cold. There was a shiver in her shoulders, running straight down her spine, but she didn't let it out. It stuck between her bones and reverberated back and forth. She took a tiny step away from him.

"What do you mean?"

He didn't say anything.

"Matthew, what are you talking about?"

He was breathing through his mouth, the skin around his lips red with rash. The tip of his nose was chapped and his eyes were really glassy. He looked up at her for a moment, then back down at the sidewalk. He shuffled his feet.

Nabila could feel her breath getting stuck in her chest. A string of white lights was blowing in the wind, and the moving shapes disoriented her. She had the urge to run, but then pushed it back down. She watched Matthew, and made herself stand very still.

"You're scaring me."

She hadn't meant to say that exactly, wasn't sure she should tell him that. But he didn't seem to think about it. He rubbed his nose. His hair was unwashed. His beard looked oily. And she realized that he had almost no control over what was happening either. Maybe he had, once, and maybe there had been a time when she would have been able to pull him out. But not here, standing with him below sea level on a cobblestone street. Things were already set.

"I'm supposed to go to that far corner, the higher ground," he said. It was just a whisper. He looked down at her, and his eyes were wide. "They said that was better, but we're pretty close. I think here's okay."

Nabila could no longer feel her hands. Everything seemed to slow down, and her legs were ready to move. She watched Matthew's face, and Matthew stared at her.

She tried to breathe, and think, and breathe, and think.

Anyone passing might think they were about to kiss. Nabila locked eyes with Matthew, and he held her gaze, kept himself steady. His eyelashes fluttered but he didn't blink.

Nabila pushed her fingers against her thigh to keep them from shaking. She could feel her heartbeat in her legs. She tried to focus on bringing air in through her nose, on keeping herself rooted to the ground. She needed to be sure.

"Why are we here?"

Matthew breathed out his mouth.

"Matthew? Please talk to me."

The skin on his face seemed too tight. His lips were exposed, his eyes were too wide. She could see his cheekbones pushing away from his jaw.

"I thought we were going to get you home so that you could start over. You wanted to go home, remember? I brought your passport. You wanted to leave. I know you weren't making that up."

It had all come out faster than she'd intended, and for a moment he looked stunned, but then he pulled his face back. "I did want to go home," he said. "But it didn't matter. There were other plans. You should leave now."

"What's in the backpack?"

He shifted the straps gently toward his neck. "Now you get it."

Nabila stared hard. "A gun?" she whispered.

Matthew nodded.

Nabila balled her hands into fists to try and ground her body. Out of the corner of her eye she worked to find a path across the street, a place that she could run to, find safety. She saw only a bus stop and a clump of trees. In the other direction, away from the street, there was the fence around the market, the front of a store and then a donair restaurant. There were cars clogging the intersection and people on the sidewalk everywhere.

"Has it really come to this?" she asked.

Matthew didn't answer. He had a Kleenex still in his hands, and he was folding and unfolding it with his thumb. His eyes went glassy, and then he sneezed. Nabila flinched.

"You have a cold."

He slowly raised the Kleenex to his face, wiped his nose. There was panic spinning around inside of Nabila, but she held it down, searched his face. His jaw was set in a way she hadn't seen before, and she wondered if he had changed, if he was different than the person she thought she knew. But beneath his wet hair and backpack, behind the frown lines that he'd twisted above his eyebrows, she could see that he was uncertain. His eyes flickered across her face, the same way they used to when he'd suggest an addition to their dinner bowl, or a shift in their rooftop shelter. He was waiting for her to decide what she thought.

Nabila breathed carefully. "You don't have to do this," she said.

"You don't know anything."

"I know this is a bad idea."

"I don't have a choice," Matthew said. "If I don't do it, they're going to hurt you." He said the last part so quietly that Nabila almost didn't hear it.

"Me?"

"They know all about you. And now you're here." He dropped his eyes. "He's watching you. I have to do it."

Nabila couldn't think straight. She could feel a panic rising in her body, telling her she needed to run, to get away. She remembered how big the bodyguard was, how mean his face looked. She didn't want to think about what he could do.

"Will you go? Please," Matthew said.

His speech was a bit slurred, Nabila realized. He had a strange dreamy look in his eyes, glazed over, detached. It worried her.

"Look, let's cross the street. Let's go over there, by those trees. We can figure things out."

"I should get it over with."

Nabila shook her head. Her panic was changing, morphing into something that was closer to anger. She crossed her arms. "So, that's it?" she said. "They can't just make you do this." Nabila heard her own voice crack.

Matthew shifted his feet. A group of teenagers walked by them, laughing loudly. Nabila watched the backpack, watched as one of the kids came within a couple of inches of it.

"I didn't mean for it to happen like this," he said.

"What did you mean to happen?"

"I don't know." Matthew was folding the Kleenex up again, looking down at the ground. "I didn't mean for any of it to happen, really. It happened slowly."

Nabila uncrossed her arms, then crossed them the other way. She saw Matthew watching her hands. She should have seen it, she thought. She should have picked up on something. But they'd been so close to getting him out.

"I'm so tired, Nabila."

Matthew looked at her and she could tell he was about to shatter. She could suddenly see how broken he was. His eye was twitching. His clothes were still wet. The Kleenex he'd been folding was starting to shred. He was leaning to one side, bending one leg, almost as if ready to fall over.

"Matthew?"

He exhaled very slowly. His hand was shaking now. He caught one finger in the strap of the backpack to steady it, and Nabila thought about how quickly it could suddenly be over if he decided to do it. She stood up straight. "Let's just cross the street, okay? Over to those trees. It'll give us some space to think."

"I don't want to think about it anymore."

His eyes were blinking furiously, and Nabila felt like she was diving and running out of air. Matthew dropped his gaze and let his chin almost touch his chest. She was losing him, Nabila realized. He didn't want to talk, and she didn't know how to distract him. She imagined the gunfire, the smell of it, the people being shot to the ground. She imagined the sirens. The news reports.

"You can't fix this, Nabila."

There were police at the entrance of the market, a couple of officers who were wearing reflective yellow. One of them looked over toward them, and Nabila tried to catch his eye, but he turned away too quickly. There were people all around, making their way down the sidewalk, cars passing on the street. She felt her breathing become shallow, felt it getting stuck in her throat.

"You haven't done anything yet, Matthew. You can choose to come home."

He shook his head, and a tiny tear slipped onto his cheek. He wiped it away immediately.

Nabila realized that she should just move. She took a small step toward him, and he didn't flinch. She moved a little bit closer, until she could see the freckles on the bridge of his nose. His nostrils flared a bit as he inhaled. She looked at him, and he looked back. "Follow me," she said.

She wasn't exactly sure what he'd do. She took a small step, and he looked as if he might reach out and grab her, tug her toward him, but he didn't. He watched her. She stepped again, and then once more, until she was almost a metre away. His eyes didn't leave her.

And then his feet shifted. They pointed toward her, and then stayed like that for a moment. Then he took a step. He pulled the backpack up on his shoulders, and she held her breath.

He came a bit closer. And then a bit more. She started walking, very slowly, and he followed. She tried not to look back. She didn't want him to question things. She wanted it to seem like she knew he would come with her.

Nabila waited until there was a gap between cars, and she started to cross the street. She forced her heartbeat down away from her throat. Matthew was walking very slowly, stepping quietly behind her. A car turned the corner and started coming toward them, and it was as if they were caught in a spotlight for a moment, captured mid-movement. She focused on the curb on the other side, sped up until she reached it. She turned around, saw Matthew still a few paces back. The car passed just behind him. Its horn blared.

There was grass on this side of the road, a bit of rain stuck on some of the blades. She could feel the slip of the wetness beneath her feet. She turned Matthew away from the bus stop, kept walking toward the patch of trees. They were on a small hill that ran down to the bank of the river. She hadn't seen the water before, but now she noticed it moving, waving. The lights from the street rippled across it in patterns.

"Nabila? Wait. Wait a minute."

"Just come on." She kept walking.

It could all be over at any moment. She imagined falling, her lungs squeezing. Her body being pushed flat into the earth.

"Nabila?"

"What?"

"I'm scared, too."

They'd reached the trees. She stopped, and turned around, and Matthew was standing there the way he'd always done in the rooftop garden, waiting for her to tell him what to do. He stared at her, then stared back at the market, shuffled his feet.

"It's okay. We're figuring this out."

He shook his head then, covered his face with his hands. His shoulders rolled forward. She should reach out, she knew, touch his elbow, say something. But another part of her wondered if she should run. She could make it back across the street, she figured, yell for people to scatter. They could try to get away.

She looked over at the police officers again, tried to catch someone's eye. This time she thought maybe one looked back at her.

Matthew pulled his hands away from his face. He sniffled. "So," he said quietly. He looked at her. "What do we do?"

"Can you take the backpack off? Let's just drop it in the river and go."

"I already told you, he's watching. He'll come after you."

"Where is he?" Nabila asked. She swivelled all around, tried to find the man from the woods but couldn't.

Matthew stared at her, and she didn't know what else to say. Then he laughed. It was a weak sound, came out as more of a wheeze. It made her nervous.

"You're too late, Nabila. It doesn't matter anymore."

"Matthew, please."

His eyes were red, and his hands were fists, pressed up against the outside of his thighs. He looked back toward the market. Nabila's fingers and legs were alive with energy. She couldn't let him go back there. She'd have to stop him.

Then there was somebody moving toward them. Nabila saw him at the edge of her vision, walking at a steady pace, crossing the street. She didn't turn her head. Matthew hadn't noticed yet, was still staring at her with a face that was quivering.

She was trying to figure out what to do. They were just out of range of the circumference of streetlights, standing between two bare trees, but were close enough to still be visible. The person was passing between cars. He was coming straight for them. And then she saw the lights reflecting off his chest, realized it was one of the police officers.

She turned back, and Matthew was squinting at her. She swallowed. He flung around to follow where her gaze had been.

Nabila took a few steps back.

The officer was stepping across the bike lane, coming up on the curb. Matthew was focused on him. He was completely still, his hands pulled tight against his sides. Nabila watched as the officer didn't slow his pace, but looked at her, then back to Matthew, then said something neither of them could understand.

Matthew whipped his head back around, settled his gaze on her. His eyes were wide and red. Then he turned back to the officer.

"Don't come closer!" he said. He was trying to shout, but his voice was giving way. Then he reached behind him and suddenly had a massive rifle in his hands.

The police officer stopped moving and held his hands away from his body. He looked at Nabila and then back to Matthew again.

"Put down the gun," he said in English.

Matthew aimed it right at him.

"Matthew, don't," Nabila said. She stepped toward one of the trees. It wouldn't protect her from much, she knew, but at least it was something. She held on to the bark.

"Put the gun down," the officer repeated.

Matthew took a few steps back, looked from Nabila back to the officer. She could see his hands shaking. "No closer!" he tried to scream, but his voice cracked.

The officer had his hand on his gun now, but kept it close to his body, still pointed toward the ground. Nabila held her breath.

Suddenly someone in the crowd across the street started screaming. People started running everywhere and then more people were yelling. Matthew moved his gun from side to side. He looked frantic.

"Stay calm, Matthew. Don't do anything fast," Nabila said.

"Leave us alone!" Matthew screamed at the officer.

She could see his legs tense, his knees bend as if he were about to run. He looked at the sidewalk across the street.

"Matthew!" Nabila called. She heard her own voice shake. "Don't do it. It's over."

He glanced at her, his teeth almost chattering, an inch of mucus trailing from his left nostril.

The officer took that moment to raise his own gun. "Your knees," he said. "On your knees."

"Nabila?" Matthew looked at her.

"Do what he says."

"I can't."

"On your knees," the officer said again. He stepped closer.

For a moment Nabila and Matthew looked at each other, bare tree branches moving in the wind above them. There was still music in the distance, swaying lights, the sound of car tires on wet pavement. Matthew looked tired. She knew he wanted her to do something, wanted her to tell him the way out.

"Nabila?" his voice cracked.

"Don't shoot," she said.

He turned around and started to run. He couldn't move very fast, was still limping, but he got behind one tree, and then another, and then came to the top of the riverbank. The officer was shouting, running after him. Nabila yelled but it was no words, just sound. She saw Matthew trip over something, a tree root, a stump, and pitch forward down the bank. There was a splash, and the officer shouted again, and Nabila ran into the road without looking.

She slipped on the lane marking, fell with her hands on the wet asphalt. She heard tires screech, saw headlights move around her, and every part of her braced for an impact. But the cars turned away from her, and she got up, made it to the other curb. People were staring.

Then there was a deep cracking sound, a roaring gunshot. The noise came at her, rushing through the air. She heard screams, saw people try to take cover. Then there were more gunshots and she heard the splash of water, of bullets landing in the river.

He fell into the water and there were rocks at the bottom and he was sure his knee was smashed. The cold of the river was a relief, attacking every part of his skin, forcing him to focus only on that pain. He kicked off the shore, pushed himself farther out. He couldn't see anything.

He kept the gun above the water, and his feet pounded against sand and old leaves. He was glad Nabila wasn't close. He'd tried his best to protect her, and he hoped it was enough. He didn't back out of the mission, he told himself. He just did a bad job of it.

The river had gotten deeper. There was shouting behind him, and he took a breath in, put his head beneath the surface to mute the world. Everything became calmer.

Matthew always remembered how Nabila loved the ocean. She loved it because it was powerful, he thought, because even though people cut down trees and bulldozed fields and left garbage in the water, the ocean could always come roaring back. It could destroy everything by just flowing and flooding. She used to think that was so amazing, he remembered, and then realized she was right. There was all this ability just beneath the surface, but you didn't always see how strong it was unless you were paying attention.

Matthew tried swimming. He let go of the gun and moved his hands through the water, kicked his feet. The effort was too much though, so instead he let himself stay still, allowed his body to be weightless near the surface. He imagined the river lapping against tree trunks and roadways, the ocean filling up concrete streets and making islands out of apartment buildings, a patch of vegetation amidst all of it growing up into the sky.

Then he felt something hit his body and it was like fire bursting through water, consuming him.

The ambulances came, but no one got in them. Some people stood on the street, watching, but most of them had listened to the police when they told them to go home. Paramedics had come by, asking if anyone was hurt, but no one was. Soon the ambulances moved farther down the street and then pulled away.

Nabila saw three different kinds of officers, all with weapons, running down toward the riverbank. One of the paramedics had given her a blanket. She stood on the sidewalk watching her hands shake beneath the blanket, watching her shoulders shiver, but she didn't feel cold. It was unnerving.

She knew things had happened quickly, but it was feeling like a long time. She couldn't quite piece together the sequence of events. Instead, she remembered snippets: the headlight of a car above her, a child's red mitten dropped on the sidewalk, the panic of multiple sirens getting closer. She tried to use those moments to fill in the gaps, but it was as if nothing existed between them. She couldn't figure out how she'd gotten to the place where she was standing now.

A police officer was there standing next to Nabila, but Nabila couldn't remember her name. She did know that they were waiting for some of the cars to pull off the road so they could go to the station. She also remembered that they wanted to know what she knew: they'd asked about Matthew, about his gun, asked if she had any part in it. She remembered herself saying no over and over again and feeling stupid.

The questions, she remembered, had been harsh. One of the officers had grabbed her shoulder while they talked as if to make sure she didn't run away. She'd never been approached like that before, seen in a way that assumed she might be guilty. She'd stood on the sidewalk and explained and explained, and she knew that she was talking too fast, that she wasn't quite convincing them. They asked for her passport and she said that it was back in her room at the café. She handed over Matthew's passport though. They took her phone, asked for the passcode, starting looking through it. They told her they needed to ask some further questions.

Nabila couldn't figure out how long they'd been waiting. She noticed that there were more officers behind her, forming a bit of a circle. They were keeping her away from other people. She could smell smoke and roasted meat, imagined that the market behind them was still cooking bratwurst over an open-air fire.

She realized that her skin was very cold. She pulled the blanket tighter across her chest but she was still shivering. The officer next to her glanced over but didn't say anything.

Someone had said that Matthew had tried to get away by swimming down the river, and that the officer had shot him. She imagined that pieces of his body would be settling on the bottom of the riverbed alongside leaves and sticks, shifting the mud.

A police car finally pulled up, and the officer next to her opened the back door and ushered Nabila inside.

They took her to a station and kept her there for a while. She didn't know how long exactly because time seemed to be moving very slowly but then suddenly all these things had happened. They'd put her in a room with a cold metal seat and asked her lots of questions. She knew it didn't look good that she was there, that she had Matthew's passport, but she just kept telling them that she didn't know what he was going to do. That she'd been trying to help a friend.

The officer questioning her got stuck on that point for a while. "But why did you want to help him?" he kept asking, and Nabila tried to explain but it was hard.

"We were really close when we were kids," she kept saying.

He didn't understand. "But that was then. This is now. He was very different from you."

Nabila could feel her voice shaking. "I know it doesn't really make sense," she said. "But he didn't have anyone else."

Then Nabila had cried, really cried, her eyes blurry and her nose dripping mucus.

The officer took a packet of tissues out of his pocket and pushed them toward her. She pulled one out and blew her nose.

"What if he'd injured people? Killed people?"

Nabila looked up. "Everyone's okay?"

He nodded. "Even the officer who chased him only has a sprained ankle. Nobody got hurt."

Nabila folded up the tissue. "Only Matthew."

They eventually let her go. She walked out the front door of the station and the wind was cold. She wrapped her scarf tighter around her neck. She wasn't sure if she was heading in the right direction.

Matthew was gone. Things had ended so quickly that she was having trouble remembering what had happened. She couldn't make sense of how the two of them had come to that point.

She walked for a while before stopping to figure out where she was. She recognized some shops, the distance from the TV tower. She realized she had to turn left. There was an old building with graffiti in different colours in front of her, a pigeon that took off from the cobblestones and landed on the edge of a roof. She was cold again. She thought she might be hungry, too.

Nabila felt something start to crack open in her belly. She kept walking, but she could feel herself start to unravel. The world had shifted and things were out of place. There had been an earthquake or a meteorite, maybe, and now there was a giant wave pushing ocean over everything. Cars would be submerged. Buildings would flood and streetlights would be washed away. She needed to find higher ground.

She turned down one street, then another. She was pretty sure she knew where she was going now, and then finally she saw the war tree, its branches waving in an invisible current. She thought of the smell of the café, of the books and coffee and wet earth. Suddenly she was very tired.

Nabila made her way up to the front door and unlocked it. Inside, things were quiet. The air was cool.

And then she couldn't stand anymore. Her knees gave way and she landed on the wooden floor with her legs curled up beneath her. She heard a gentle thud, but couldn't connect the sound of the impact to her body.

The door had slammed shut; the sound had been loud, and she waited as the room decayed.

There was one time, up on the roof, when they had been playing outside and it had started pouring rain. The sky had gotten suddenly dark, almost like night. The wind was whipping the branches of the sandbar willows around. The raindrops were so big that they hurt when they landed on her cheek.

Tara Lynn had bundled up Samir and run inside toward the elevators, but then had stood at the glass door, calling for Nabila and Matthew to join them. Matthew had wanted to go in. He was getting really wet, he'd told Nabila, but it had been so mesmerizing, being that close to the clouds, watching as the wind pushed them across the sky, that Nabila didn't want to move. There was a roar to the rain that drowned out everything else. She remembers throwing her hands into the air and laughing.

Matthew and Tara Lynn had both been calling her name. Matthew had also come right up next to her, was pulling at the edge of her sleeve. But she was spellbound.

When she finally did go in, Tara Lynn had yelled until Samir started to cry. She'd made Nabila and Matthew stand at the entrance to the apartment until she brought them towels. Nabila hadn't cared, but Matthew couldn't look at any of their faces. He'd just shivered and blinked the water out of his eyes.

"Why didn't you just go inside?" she remembers snapping at him.

They were still towelling off their hair when Matthew's sisters had buzzed from downstairs. It was only afterwards, after she'd stood under a warm shower and had a cup of hot milk at the kitchen table, that Nabila thought about how Matthew would have had to walk home in the rain. He never had an umbrella, and if his sisters did, they probably wouldn't have shared. When he got home, nobody would have helped him get warm.

That was the day Nabila learned how fast the sky could move, and how she could push boundaries and always be taken care of. And it was the day, she realized now, that explained to her why Matthew couldn't do that. She imagined him following his sisters into their apartment, taking off his wet shoes, trying to wrap himself in a blanket.

Nabila put her hands down on the floor and pushed herself up. She was dizzy for a moment, her head spinning, but then she steadied. Her eyes focused and she could see the shape of tables in the dark, the outline of books. There were vines snaking across the wall.

Things weren't okay. They couldn't ever be, really. But that didn't change the fact that she had to lock the door behind her, test the handle, walk quietly across the room to the back hallway.

The room with the war tree was dark, but she could see the outline of its shape in the middle. She went up to it and touched its side, then put her arms around it, rested her cheek against the bark. She felt stable then, and felt how alone it must be without any other trees like it, its roots crawling through the ground, desperately searching, trying to find other roots to rely on. She thought about how deeply it must be hurting.

Matthew had died trying to protect her. She didn't think there were many people in the world who would have done that. Her parents, and maybe her brother. And Matthew. She wouldn't have expected that from him, wasn't sure he would have been capable, or that he'd want to. But he had.

There was quiet laughter from upstairs, and Nabila could tell it was Tierney, knew that she and Ricardo were probably in the kitchen or in Tierney's room. She didn't want to talk to them, but liked knowing they were there. It made her less lonely.

She thought about how she would leave tomorrow, fly back to her basement lab that smelled of ocean in the middle of the city, to her canisters of seaweed. She'd go for drinks with her work friends, and they'd ask about her trip and she'd say it was great. She'd tell them about the museums, but she wouldn't mention Matthew. How could she tell that story? They wouldn't understand. Nabila didn't even understand.

Now she could only think of her and Matthew in terms of their imagined world, their failures in the real one. It only made sense to her to remember the two of them on a rooftop overlooking the city, creating a place where they were safe. And they were safe there, she knew, safe and together. It was what they'd had before the rest of the world rushed in.

EPILOGUE

November wasn't the best time of year to plant a tree, but it was still warm enough and the soil hadn't frozen yet. Nabila was on the roof of the university's botany building. It wasn't very high, just a few storeys up, and the sounds from the street were still loud. Nabila had to work to block them out.

Most of the plants on the roof were small: thin cedars, some prairie grass, a garden where there would be rows of lettuce and tomatoes in summer. They didn't want anything too tall, the director had told her, but there was some spare soil that would support a small sandbar willow. They probably wouldn't use it for research, he'd said, but if she wanted to plant it, there was a square plot of empty space she could have.

Nabila had bought the tree and had carried it up the four flights of stairs because there were too many people using the elevator. She was sweating. Up on the roof, the wind whipped around the branches and one of them almost poked her in the eye.

There were garden tools in a small shed, and she took out a shovel and started digging until she had a hole that was big enough. Then she unwrapped the roots from their burlap and laid them in the soil. They wouldn't be able to grow deep, she saw, but they had a bit of space to grow wide, and that should be enough for them to hang on.

She shovelled dirt back around the trunk and then turned on the hose. As the soil around its base became moist, gentle rain began to fall. So she removed the hose and then patted down some of the earth that had become loose. At first she hadn't been sure if planting a tree would help, but now she knew that Matthew would have liked it, and that it would be good for her, too. She already felt calmer.

Above her, the clouds had gotten thick and the rain, she understood, would last for a while. It was already drowning out the noises of the city. She stood there next to the tree and touched its branches, listened for the sound of the raindrops hitting the soil. Then she stared up into the sky and waited for it to pour.

ACKNOWLEDGEMENTS

I started writing this book seven years ago, and there have been so many people who have been a part of this process.

To Grace, for being the best friend and travel buddy to explore Berlin with. Thank you for our work sessions in Prenzlauer Berg cafés, and for answering all of my random questions about urban plants!

Thank you to everyone who has read my work over the years and helped me develop my writing, especially within the University of Toronto's creative writing program. To other writers who've inspired and encouraged me, including Danila, Ian and Kevin. To my sister Nalini and aunt Cathy for being my first readers and editors. And to Nahlah, for your continued encouragement and mentorship.

My writing is only where it is today because of Camilla's guidance. Thank you for your kindness, insights, mentorship and friendship.

To Nightwood Editions, especially Silas and Emma, for your belief in this story. To my amazing editor, Karlene, for your astute suggestions, and publicist Annie, for your help getting this book out into the world. Also thanks to Angela for the beautiful cover design.

To Alex, and all of my extended family. Thank you for your love, your excitement about my writing, and your patience and understanding when I need to work.

And finally, thank you to Nalini, Mom and Dad. I'm so grateful for your encouragement, support and endless belief in me, no matter what I choose to do. None of this would have been possible without you.

PHOTO CREDIT: FRED LUM

ABOUT THE AUTHOR

Menaka Raman-Wilms is a writer and journalist based in Toronto. She's the host of *The Decibel*, the daily news podcast from *The Globe and Mail*. Previously, she was a parliamentary reporter for *The Globe and Mail* and an associate producer at CBC Radio One. She has a master's in creative writing from the University of Toronto and a master's in journalism from Carleton University. She's also a classically trained singer. For several years, Menaka reviewed books for the *Ottawa Review of Books*, and has moderated panel discussions at Ottawa's Prose in the Park literary festival. In 2019, Menaka's story "Black Coffee" was shortlisted for the CBC Short Story Prize. She received the youth award at the Alice Munro Festival of the Short Story in 2016, and won *Room Magazine*'s 2012 fiction contest. Her work has also been published in *Broken Pencil Magazine* and *Acta Victoriana*.